THE
SHACKLE

escape from the knot of restraint

The KNOT Series unfolds romantic drama as good trumps evil, using the themes of art, tennis and Texas ranching. The novels untangle struggles and interlock friendships as the main characters achieve emotional healing and self-confidence on their journey to find love.

THE KNOT SERIES I

The Trinity Knot
The Zeppelin Bend (sequel to *The Trinity Knot*)
The Hitch (sequel to *The Zeppelin Bend*)

THE KNOT SERIES II

The Shackle (sequel to *The Hitch*)

THE
SHACKLE

escape from the knot of restraint

DONNALEE
OVERLY

The Shackle Copyright © 2020 by DonnaLee Overly

For permission, please contact the author at
 www.donnaleeoverly.com or e-mail donnaleeoverly@gmail.com.

Printed in the United States of America
First Edition, October 2020

Cover and Interior design by Roseanna White Designs
The Shackle Knot artwork by DonnaLee Overly

Library of Congress Control Number: 2020911619

ISBN Trade Paperwork- 13: 978-1-7352517-0-7
 E-BOOK: 13: 978-1-7352517-1-4

www.donnaleeoverly.com

*The majority of this manuscript was written
during the 2020 Stay at Home order
so I would like to dedicate this book
to the people around the world
who died during the corona pandemic
and to the victims of human trafficking.*

*"The greatest thing in the world
is to know how to belong to oneself."*

~ Michel Eyquem de Montaigne (1533-1592)

PART 1

CHAPTER 1

Rolling onto her back with the hard earth beneath, Marie is grateful for the thick cloud cover that will soon hide the stars. After performing the ritual of the sign of the cross, her eyes close, hoping to end this nightmare, but the heaviness of her breathing and the aching of her body scream that this is all too real.

Even though the twenty-six-year-old fought hard, a fight that would have made any parent proud, the wetness traveling down her cheeks cries despair. These past twenty-four hours have been horrific but for now she has successfully escaped her capturers. It's as if she's in an adventure film; however, unlike the film on the big screen, no Indiana Jones has come to her rescue.

Recalling the events of the past week, she releases a muffled cry, haunted by images racing in her brain of the terror on Alexa's face as their kidnappers dragged her away. Surely, Marie could have done something to help save her best friend. Her stomach churns, and she realizes she's going to vomit.

A few weeks earlier, Marie Gomez and Alexa Roberts arrived in Cancun for a well-earned vacation, to celebrate their recent graduation with their master's degrees. Walking the vibrant, colorful streets of the Mexican town one evening, their fun plans turned upside-down. There was a screech of tires, and then noise of van doors opening and men rushing. The ordeal happened so fast that the events that followed remain scrambled in her mind. But Marie recalls quite clearly that after traveling two days in a hot, dark trailer over bumpy roads, their kidnappers opened the door, before placing cloth bags over their heads, and then dragging them as they were too weak to walk at the fast pace.

That's the last she knew of her friend's whereabouts. Alexa is beautiful with shoulder-length long blond hair and a bombshell body. The picture of the perfect Eve. Marie had listened as Alexa's screams got fainter and then finally stopped. Alas, that was more than a week ago.

Now, lying face down in the dirt and exhausted, Marie imagines her best friend's fate— raped...drugged...killed? No, these men would not kill Alexa as that would make this whole kidnapping senseless. What have they done with her best friend?

As she takes a deep breath, a sharp pain rips across her left side causing tears to stream off her chin. She must have bruised her side when she stumbled and fell on some rocks. Her escape had her crawling under thickets and wading through creek beds. Running her tongue over her dry, cracked lips, she tastes blood. The blood doesn't matter, nothing matters. She has exhausted all of her strength and wit to escape, knowing her fate if caught will involve stiff punishment and maybe even her life. However, determined to be brave, she'd rather fight than be a pawn in their games of drug smuggling and human trafficking.

For now, there's no more running, not one small step. She can't crawl or claw her way another inch. She's done. Her wet clothes cling to her body and she shivers. During her prayers for herself and Alexa, the darkness wins the battle.

CHAPTER 2

One month earlier

Opening the door to the Jeep, Stan Adams motions with a jerk of his head for the mutt to climb aboard; however, the borador—a border collie / black lab mix—cocks his head as if questioning with a look of complete bewilderment. The black markings near his eyes make him appear sad, and that forces Stan to take pity and chuckle at the same time.

"Okay, boy, so I'm guessing that your past didn't include riding with your head hanging out the window in the breeze. What was in your past? Lord only knows." He pats the dog on the head and that seems to calm the animal. "Today your past is just that, the past. Done. Today, you're moving forward." The dog rolls his ears back and continues to stare with big questioning eyes.

At the moment, it isn't clear if Stan is referring to his new companion's former life or to his own. Having one's heart broken takes a toll. Daily, he observes the woman who stole his heart with another man and that disturbs him more than facing his own death.

He's trying like hell to move forward. He's been trying for the past few months, but telling his soul and mind to stop loving remains an impossible feat. Each day he begins with a new mindset; then something triggers that buried yearning. Whether a phone call, or a silly phrase, or a blond stranger walking down the sidewalk, anything that points a degree toward Gabby reopens the wound, causing his heart to hemorrhage. He's been patching this wound with a Band-Aid, and after one of his mandated visits to the psychiatrist as part of his release agreement from drug rehab, the doc suggested that a pet might just be the perfect fix for his injured heart. It's likely Stan needs saving more than the friend he adopted from the rescue center.

The doc explained that the responsibilities of owning a pet should curb Stan's expressed loneliness by providing a sense of purpose, along with the benefit of a companion who would listen without offering unsolicited advice.

"It's you and me now, boy." Stan scratches his head thinking about a catchy name for his friend. He can't keep calling him "boy."

"You'll be begging for rides before too long." He picks up the twenty-four-pound borador and sets him on the back seat. The dog's weight for his age of three years is low and his coat thin, but the veterinarian familiar with rescues, reassured Stan that with steady, proper nutrition, the lab will gain both weight and strength quickly.

Assessing the dog's uneasiness, he says, "Hey, boy, it's gonna be okay. I promise." The dog whimpers, a sorrowful sound as if voicing Stan's innermost woes.

Shaking his head, Stan leans into the Jeep, gathers the dog to his chest, and buries his face into its fur before opening the driver's door.

"All right, shotgun, is that better?" The dog barks as if he agrees. *What am I getting myself into?* Stan wonders.

A former attorney with a big Washington law firm, he had a horrendous motorcycle accident last year. He'd moved to Texas to be with family who offered assistance during his healing—his mother, Rita Adams King, and her husband, Texas oil and cattle rancher Wayne King. Stan had sustained a broken arm and a totally busted left leg, the reason he limps.

Now thirty-four years old, he is a muscular guy with a slightly receding hairline. On a good day he doesn't use his cane, but with overuse or cold weather, the pain gets the better of him and the crutch does provide relief. In the beginning, he took pills for the pain, many pills there for a while. These made the pain in his leg tolerable, but they also helped to dull his aching heart. The overused drugs landed him in the rehabilitation center for six weeks. After exhausting the alternative pain relief measures, he still relies on Tylenol and at times alcohol when the pain's unbearable. However, he's tough and determined, and has trouble accepting that he allowed weakness to control his battle. He loathes weakness and vows never to reach that low point again.

So, he keeps on track without narcotics and with his weekly appointments to the psychiatrist. He believes they're friends. After crashing his bike and convalescing in Texas, the stinging truth revealed that he doesn't have many friends. It's mostly his pride that keeps him from maintaining any past friendships. His injuries required months of physical therapy and it was uncertain if he would ever walk again. His ego grieves the loss of his former active lifestyle, even though it is short of a miracle that he can walk with just the assistance of a cane.

Many unforeseen changes came after the accident, but today the decision to adopt a dog is a positive move. He's had enough bad karma, combined with self-destructive behavior. Adopting this scrawny rescue starts his new proactive plan. The Jeep's engine roars, startling the dog, causing him to stand at attention with a nervous, bewildered face. Stan reaches his hand across the console to steady his nervous passenger. *Am I as fragile as this dog?*

Before placing the Jeep into gear, he picks up his phone to text his mother and give her the heads-up that he won't be home for dinner. Dinner at the ranch, a two-hour drive from his current location, is a family tradition. He'll miss dinner tonight because he has errands. First, he'll stop for pet supplies, then he'll stop at a café with dog-friendly outdoor seating, giving them a chance to get acquainted and for him to give a proper name to his new companion.

Turning onto the freeway, he leaves his window open to enjoy the cooler air of the early February evening. The dog has his head resting on his front paws as he peers out of the window. It seems that the steady motion of the drive has taken the edge off his anxiety. Realizing the dog has relaxed gives Stan hope and reassurance that the future will be brighter for both of them.

CHAPTER 3

"Stan, you soon getting finished? We can ride back to the ranch together."

Stan's gaze leaves the paperwork before him on the desk and his eyes rest on Gabby, the owner of the sweet voice, the same beautiful tone that fills his dreams at night. He rubs his forehead and his lips turn upward. He's certain that the only thing that would stop his soul from rejoicing every second the woman he loves comes within arm's reach would be if he ceased to breathe.

Gabriella is the daughter of Wayne King, and since Stan's mother and King married, Gabby officially became his stepsister. However, just four short months ago when Stan was doing his stint in rehab, Gabby tied the knot with Brett Matthews. The couple had met at the country club where Brett was a tennis professional. Back then he had quite a reputation as a "bad boy." Initially, she'd steered clear of him; however, over time everything changed. Then, shortly after they started dating, Brett quit the club and began working at the King ranch as a wrangler.

Stan is convinced that if he had met Gabby first, he would have won her affection. Brett is an okay guy, but Stan doesn't see why women swoon over him. Could it be that his handsome face masks any flaw in his personality? But since Stan's accident brought him to Texas, he's painfully watched Gabby and Brett's relationship grow. Now she wears his ring and it's Brett she holds at night. Why didn't Gabby realize that Stan was the better choice? Quite frankly, it sucks that she chose Brett.

Gabby, lean and tall, stands in the doorway to his office at the Equine Center, where she and Stan both work with the Equine Assisted Therapy (EAT) Program. She flips her blond hair over her shoulder. He turns away. Does she understand that, when she tosses her hair with that twinkle in her brown eyes lighting her angelic face, she has the power of a surgeon whose scalpel cuts through his heart? To hide his struggle, he pretends interest in the ledger before him, tapping his fingers on the desk.

As if on cue, the heartache transfers to his leg and he rubs it. "Give me ten minutes to finish this order."

She smiles. "Not a problem but beware—Jamie hates when we're late for dinner. I'll pull the truck up to the door, so you don't have far to walk." He throws her the keys.

Of course, she offered to bring the truck to the entrance after observing him rub his leg. That is who she is, thoughtful and kind. *Does she compare pathetic Stan to her strong, confident husband?*

Before exiting she says, "Oh, by the way, Ella says hi. And that she and Will are doing great. They miss you."

"Oh, thanks. How's the pregnancy?" He looks up.

"All seems well. She is now seven months along."

"Thanks," he says again, not looking up as Gabby leaves the room.

Ella, Gabby's best friend from college, is married to Will, Stan's younger brother. When they met it was as if fireworks were set off; wed shortly thereafter, they now have a child on the way. They live in Washington, DC.

"Damn," he utters under his breath as he rubs his leg again.

"Time to go, Ryder." Hearing his name, Ryder shakes his head as Stan hears the dog's tags jingle. Ryder naps in the adjacent room as he prefers the heat emitted from the motor of the mini-fridge over the cramped small space under Stan's desk. Usually he wakes and greets a visitor but failed to acknowledge Gabby's visit. Maybe Ryder has a better sense of what Stan needs than Stan does.

Gathering his papers, he places an appointment schedule and some bills in his leather pouch; lastly, he tucks an old yellowed map into the front cover of his notebook for safekeeping and adds it to the pouch. He'll finish this at home. Reaching for his cane, he works his way from behind the desk and pours the remaining water from his Yeti cup into the dog's dish. Ryder laps it up and raises his eyes in gratitude.

"You're a good dog. Ready to go home?" He pets Ryder, who nods as if he understands Stan's struggle. "You're smart too. Don't let a female ruin you, promise?"

The honk of the horn brings Gabby back to mind. Reaching for his hat, he turns off the light and closes the door. His companion follows at his heels as the horn blasts a second time. He slows his gait. *Yeah, yeah, I can take my time. Good old Brett can just wait. He'd wait a lifetime for Gabby. Any man would.*

Approaching the truck, he opens the back door and Ryder hops in without hesitation. As always, his friend anticipates rides, the reason for his name. Stan also tosses his cane into the back.

"I'm driving, pretty lady." He waves a thumb suggesting that Gabby move away from the driver's seat.

She pushes out her lower lip, then smiles. "Okay, your call." She slides across the bench seat to the passenger side.

"Buckle up, girl, 'cause we're going for a nice ride. Ryder likes to go fast, don't you, boy?" At the mention of his name, the pup places his head over the back of the front seat.

Gabby gives him a pat. "Such a sweet boy. So it's Ryder who likes to go fast." She winks at Stan. "I see." She pulls on the strap tightening her seatbelt. "Okay then. It's fortunate he found our family. Reminds me of someone."

The engine revs and the truck spins out on the gravel drive, spitting stones and dust. Gabby giggles.

Stan glances her way and grins. God, he loves the sound of her laugh. He imagines the chimes of a thousand tiny bells.

****

Before the truck comes to a complete stop in front of the ranch house, Brett jumps off the wide porch that encircles the house. He opens Gabby's door and pulls her out of the truck and plants a kiss on her lips, lifting her feet up off the ground and swirling her around.

"I thought you'd never get home. I have good news. No, make that great news."

At times, Brett is like an excited kid in a grown man's body. His face beams at the thought of a surprise.

"What is it?" She tilts her head to study his face in search of a clue.

"Can't tell you. I need to show you. Come along." He pulls on her arm. "Jamie packed our dinner so we can get on our way."

Jamie and Rusty Jones have worked the King ranch for nearly three decades. Rusty is the ranch foreman and Jamie's in charge of the household and cooks for the ranch hands. The Kings consider them family.

Stan's intense stare catches Brett's attention, so Brett holds up a picnic basket. "Oh, hi, Stan. Did you have a good day at the horse center?"

Stan attaches the leash to Ryder's collar to avoid any further eye contact. "Yeah, it was great." His tone attempts to match their joyful one but his shoulders droop.

"Bye, Ryder. Thanks, Stan. See you tomorrow," Gabby calls over her shoulder.

Skeptical, Stan watches them stroll away arm-in-arm with the basket swaying in tempo. He wonders what boyish scheme Brett's concocted. It is Wednesday and weekdays around the ranch are fairly typical. He recalls nothing from recent conversations that would cause such fervor. What could be so important? King respects the idea of family and it's an unwritten rule that dinnertime is a tradition.

Gabby waves as the red convertible zooms past. Immediately Stan's limp becomes more pronounced, reminding him to retrieve his cane from the back seat of the truck.

He travels slowly up the wooden ramp that King installed last year when Stan was wheelchair-bound, but today that doesn't make him feel special. The cane thumps hard with each step on the wooden structure and he prays for a heart made of the same.

The swish of a furry tail against his leg brings him back to the present.

"Come on, Ryder. Let's see about dinner." The dog licks his hand and leans in closer as if he understands.

CHAPTER 4

A short time later, the red BMW convertible pulls into the circular drive of the recently built Matthews residence. Gabby's daddy gave her two acres on the southeast side of the ranch, across from the lake. Construction of her dream house started right away after her engagement to Brett in August. Six months later the newlyweds moved into their love nest, a sprawling one-story ranch built with natural stone and painted in earth tones to blend into the surroundings. Adding the tennis court and swimming pool completed the homestead and made it uniquely perfect for them.

Brett opens the car door for Gabby, and she hands him the basket. "This is going to be so awesome," he says as he drags her toward the pool near the back of the house.

"Brett, what's going on?"

"You'll see. You'll see real soon." He ushers her through the gate. Placing the picnic basket on the table he starts to strip. First, he kicks off his boots, then tosses his clothing in all directions.

"What are you doing?" She gestures with her hand raised. "You're crazy. It's February—even in Texas, it's too cold for a swim."

"Hurry up." He motions for her to join him, grinning as wide as the Rio Grande. He's now in the buff, his muscular tanned frame heading to the edge of the pool. He turns around to check if she is following his example and motions her forward, then dives into the clear water and resurfaces on the other side.

"It's awesome." He shakes his head, spraying water droplets into the air. "Hurry up, princess. Surely, you aren't going to let me skinny-dip alone. Get your pretty butt in here or I'll come and fetch you."

"You wouldn't."

"Oh, yes, I would." Using his strong arms, he easily lifts out of the water onto the poolside and runs toward her.

"Brett, no, stop."

Holding her the way a groom would hold his bride to carry her across the threshold, in spite of her protests he carries her to the poolside.

When it's obvious that he is true to his word, she screams, "Don't you dare."

"Wrong words, princess, you know I love a dare." His eyes twinkle like stars on an emerald-green sky.

"It's cold and you'll get me all wet." She giggles and holds on tight.

"That's the idea."

She's aware that he isn't joking and prepares for the cold, wet shock. "Brett, stop."

With a giant leap, they make a splash. She wants to be angry with him but he is so darn cute with that smile that makes his dimple more pronounced. Much to her surprise, the water is as warm as a tepid bath.

He wipes her smeared mascara off her cheeks. In seconds he has shifted from the little boy to a man with desire. His kisses leave her breathless and eager for more. Gently, pushing her back against the side of the pool, she knows what he has in mind. His breath, hot against her cheek, as he unbuckles her belt and slides her pants to her knees. She searches his emerald eyes and she softens under his gaze. She craves his touch, equally sharing his desire. The cares of the world are forgotten, as they become one.

It was this undeniable chemistry, this inexplicable magic, that brought these two opposites together. Many heads turned as onlookers watched their promiscuous tennis pro capture the heart of the educated, reserved daughter of Wayne King. Their love affair in this small Texas town was front and center and caused much tongue-wagging as if the couple held the status of royalty.

After their lovemaking Brett says, "An initiation was in order, our first swim. Isn't this great? The contractor put the propane tank in early this morning and the heater has been running all day. I've been checking it every few hours and it was a cozy ninety degrees according to our new cool duck thermometer. I remember that you liked your pool water as warm as a bath."

She turns to see a yellow plastic duck wearing black sunglasses merrily bobbing along.

"Here we are on a sunny February afternoon swimming, totally awesome, right?" He's still gleaming and holding her tight.

"Totally awesome," she repeats.

Their naked, slippery bodies entwine, and he carries her moving slowly and seductively through the water. She wraps her finger around a wet brown curly lock.

"What if somebody's watching?" she whispers.

"Let them watch. Really, Scarlett, I don't give a damn." Using his best Rhett Butler imitation, he nibbles her ear and pulls her body tight against his muscles. "How's my impression?"

"Purrrfect." She closes her eyes and smiles.

Periodically he steals kisses between singing the words to his made-up impromptu song. "I'm in heaven. Holding my baby. Swimming in February in a heated pool. I'm in heaven."

Still moving in small circles, he says, "This is the life. This is our life, you and me, here together. I love you, Gabby." He nuzzles her neck. "I love you more than I ever thought possible. Do you know what makes this day special?" His eyes lock in on her brown orbs.

Before she can answer, he splashes her face with water making her squint. "It's our four-month wedding anniversary!" He splashes her again and yells, "Water fight. You're it." Diving below the surface, he's gone.

She leans back until the back of her head reaches the water and pulls her hair away from her face. Her heart rejoices. She loves him and delights in small moments like this when he exposes the sentimental side that he hides beneath his macho facade. Usually she is the one who remembers dates; today, she had been so caught up with work at the Equine Center that she had forgotten their monthly milestone. Has it really been four months since she said, "I do"?

It's her turn to tag so she dives under the surface, racing toward his lean, strong body. He willingly allows her to catch him and in their playfulness, time escapes. Hours later with fingers and toes that resemble raisins, and their growling stomachs, a glance toward the picnic basket reminds them of the forgotten dinner.

CHAPTER 5

Back at the main house, after watching the convertible until it is out of sight, Stan puts water in Ryder's dish from the hose and bids his friend to stay on the porch.

"Hello," Stan yells as he opens the front door. The rich aroma of food wets his mouth and Jamie requests that he join her in the kitchen. At this time of the day, it's unusual that the dining room table isn't set for dinner. Something's up. *Could this be part of the surprise?*

Rusty is seated at the small kitchen table. "There you are. We almost started without you. It's torture for a hungry soul. I tried stealing a dumpling, but Rita slapped my hand, said I'm being rude." The older man chuckles and motions for Stan to take a seat.

Stan scans the room. The table's set for only three. "Where's everyone?"

"As you saw, Gabby and Brett are off to their house. Seems that Brett wished to surprise Gabby with a heated pool. The propane tank was hooked up today."

After learning the reason for Brett's urgency, Stan looks away, gnaws on his lip as he washes his hands at the sink. Walking towards the table, he pulls out a chair next to Rusty as Jamie places a large serving bowl of chicken and dumplings in the center of the table. The steam sends a savory smell that helps take the edge off his feeling of abandonment.

Jamie heaps a hearty portion on his plate. "Your mother and King decided to spend the night at their condo in the city. He has a business meeting in the morning and Rita's going to take the morning shift at ArtSmart. She's talking about working the afternoon shift as well, to give the girls a well-deserved break. The gallery's doing great and they've been working extra hours since Gabby only works part-time now. Rita wants to reward them with some time off." She wipes her mouth on the napkin. "Besides, she's behind on her paperwork—something about getting a schedule of featured artists for the year. If I recall her words—there are too many distractions here."

Jamie seems to have noticed Stan's quiet demeanor and pats his hand. "We'll have a nice dinner here ourselves. I'm making your favorite dish tomorrow night: pot-roast with potatoes and that carrot casserole that you like. And how about a lemon meringue pie?" She grins. "Sounds good, right?"

Rusty pipes up, "Hey, what about my favorite? What does a husband have to do to get his favorite meal?"

"I make your favorites all the time, silly man. Besides, you love lemon meringue." She leans over and pecks him on the cheek. "You're so spoiled."

Being witness to a love that has lasted decades, Stan feels like a fifth wheel. Hunger is not the cause of the pit in his stomach; the emptiness stems from loneliness. He says, "Jamie, there's no need to make a fuss."

"I love fussing over folks that I love." Her tender look implies that she has the key giving her access to his soul. There's no fooling a wise woman on matters of the heart. Was he that transparent?

The conversation for the main course of the meal is routine. However, when Jamie serves peach pie topped with a scoop of vanilla ice cream, Rusty asks, "Where's Ryder?"

"He's out on the porch," Stan says.

"This time of year, temperatures drop fast after sunset. I'll bring him inside." Rusty stands. "I like having a dog at my feet. You picked a good one. He's smart and he took to the ranch quickly. He'll be a great help with the cattle. That's if you're still here for the spring round-up. He's good with the basic commands like sit, down and stay, so I started teaching him different whistles and hand gestures. Next week, I'm going bring some cattle into the corral. Let me know if you want to help. You need to learn too."

Rusty props his elbows on the table and leans forward. "What are your plans, Stan?"

"What?" Stan sits erect in his chair.

"Your plans...what are your plans for next year? You're a young man with tons of life to live. Not like us old folks." Rusty winks at Jamie. "Most of the medical stuff from your accident is behind you."

"Oh, I don't know." Stan rubs his head. "Getting this far has been a challenge. I rented my condo in DC until the end of summer, so I have a few months to decide." He shifts his weight in the chair.

"You and Gabby are doing some great work with the folks at the Equine Center. Jamie and I are very proud of what you're doing there."

"Thanks for saying that, and it's wonderful to help others. And they seem to trust me as one who has been there and understands what they are going through. Horseback riding has helped me rehab more quickly. I had lost tons of muscle tone from the months sitting in the wheelchair. Riding horseback takes more muscles then I ever imagined, and it's great to work out without realizing it. Not to mention, you're in nature's playground, feeling the wind on your face and hearing the birds, plus riding on an awesome animal. Sure beats a workout in the gym."

He wipes his mouth with the napkin and pushes his chair back from the table. "Combining the center with the veterans program was genius. Now the stable won't foreclose. Just worked the numbers. For the first time since opening, it's turning a profit. More doctors are using us for their patients, plus the grant money really helps. Gabby's great at applying for grants."

"That's all such good news," Rusty replies.

Gabby had gotten the idea for the center last year from Stan's friends, Andrew Green and Eric Lang, who operated a riding therapy program in Virginia.

"None of this would have been possible if you hadn't introduced Gabby to those guys. We have you to thank for that," Rusty says. He pushes his chair away from the table. "I'll go and fetch Ryder." Rusty nods before leaving the room.

Jamie reaches across the table and holds Stan's hand in a motherly fashion. "Rusty's right, you know. You have your whole life ahead. I'm glad we have this time to chat." She takes in a deep breath and stirs her coffee. "I see you watching them. And I'm sorry."

"I don't want your pity." He throws his shoulders back and sits straighter in his chair.

"I'm trying to be your friend, Stan. Your mother is thrilled to have you here but I'm not sure it's best for you." Her eyes scan his face, and no matter how difficult, he's determined to maintain eye contact. "It helps that they moved into their new house, gives you some breathing room but working so close with Gabby at the center has to be a challenge. You work there, you see her; when you're here, you see Brett. It creates a difficult situation." She pauses. "I see the pain you try to hide. Your mother doesn't want to admit it exists, but I see it."

Stan swallows hard. The thought of others witnessing and giving words to his pain causes him to look away as he exhales a long breath. "Thanks for caring. I haven't figured it out yet." His voice breaks on the last word. He's lovesick and broken. He hasn't fooled anyone, especially not the wise soul sitting next to him.

"If there is anything either Rusty or I can do for you, you just ask." She stands and, from behind his chair, wraps her arms around him.

With his eyes about to overflow with tears, his manhood is saved as Ryder rushes between them and places his paws on Stan's thighs and barks. His companion's sincere brown eyes reflect trust and loyalty, lightening Stan's darkness.

"Hey there, did Uncle Rusty let you in? How about a treat? You want a treat?" He pets Ryder with a hand rich in gratefulness.

Rusty opens the pantry. "I already got that covered. I promised him as soon as I let him in the door, and you have to follow through on promises. Ain't that right?" He offers Ryder his hand to shake, which the dog does obediently. Rusty pets him before offering the treat. Stan forces a smile.

"Thanks, Jamie. Dinner was great. Tonight, I'll dream about that pot roast, but I'm beat. This aching leg begs for a rest." He stands and grabs the cane hanging from the back of the chair.

"Come along, Boss." The dog barks and wags his tail and follows Stan up the curved stairs. The psychiatrist was right. Stan's glad he took the advice to heart. Having Ryder by his side makes his loneliness a bit easier. He'll keep Jamie's words close. Maybe Jamie's right too—it could be time to move on.

CHAPTER 6

Stan slowly hobbles up the stairs, relying heavily on the railing, to the bedroom that Gabby vacated a month ago when she and Brett officially moved out of the main ranch house and into their house. Before that, King's office had provided a makeshift bedroom, which he occupied after his accident while he was wheelchair-bound.

Gabby had taken with her all the furnishings from this room. A fresh coat of tan paint and new curtains had removed any trace of the former décor. He likes that the room is located in the front of the house. At night with the fairly flat Texas landscape, headlights are visible from the traffic a mile away on the main road. Still, he enjoys the other sounds of the night best, mostly the frogs croaking and coyotes howling.

He flops down on the bed and stares at the glow in the dark stars covering the ceiling. His mother offered to repaint the ceiling, but he opted to keep the stars. Stargazing was something he shared with Gabby and it stuck. Frequently she made wishes upon stars, and now Stan has adopted that habit as well, a bittersweet reminder.

Ryder barks as if asking to join him on the bed. When he first brought Ryder home, he placed him in a crate, but now he welcomes his friend onto his bed. He pats the comforter and the dog quickly responds, then licks Stan's face before settling down by his side. Stan places his arm around him and buries his face into the soft, cream-and-black fur. As predicted by the vet, Ryder's fur has thickened and he gained weight quickly with proper care and nutrition. Tonight, Stan's in need of a friend and with his companion by his side, it's not long before he drifts off in sleep.

With a startle, he's awake. Checking his clock, it's only 11 p.m. He napped for about two hours and that's left him feeling wide-eyed and refreshed. Ryder lifts his head as if to say *Hey, I'm sleeping, buddy*, and closes his eyes again. Stan stretches and then peers out the window in search of the stars. They're there, bright and twinkling. *Is Gabby gazing at these same stars?*

After his normal bedtime routine of a shower and brushing his teeth, he's alert and far from sleep. He could never understand the use of peppermint in toothpaste, as well as the woody fresh scent of soap. He guesses that manufacturers believe all people must shower in the morning. He may as well get something productive done to take his mind off his troubles. Reading's usually the trick that will cause his eyelids to close. Searching for something to read, he remembers the treasure, the old yellowed map in his leather pouch.

Eyeglasses in hand, and propping his foot on a stool for comfort, he carefully unfolds the map on his desk. It's old and has some tears at the creases and it needs handling with care. Since returning from rehab, his sleep patterns have been erratic. On another sleepless night similar to tonight, he browsed through the books in King's office library and this map slipped out of a history book that looked to be as old as the map. On first glance, he recognized the property lines and topography of the King ranch. But what piqued Stan's curiosity was the notation of an airstrip. Outlined on the map, near the northeast border, was a narrow area just beyond the ridge near the cliff where he and Brett rescued the trapped cattle last fall.

Now, he stares at the map and the word *Airstrip,* handwritten in ink. This marked area is remote, as it's on the far edge of the ranch, and because of the rough terrain there's little reason to travel there. His eyebrows raise and he rubs his chin. *Interesting!*

Over the past few months, Stan has driven the perimeter of the property several times while using his drone to check on the condition of the fences. It's one of several efforts he's made to gain credibility with King and prove that he isn't a complete loser. Now thinking back, even last October when he helped Brett find and rescue the missing cattle, he didn't notice anything in the landscape that would indicate an airstrip, but he wasn't looking so maybe it could have been there incognito. This is a mystery requiring an investigation. Later he'll review the video footage from his drone runs that are saved on his computer.

After studying the map in more detail, he takes a photo of it with his cell phone for future reference. In addition, he measures the distances from familiar landmarks so that he'll have reference points to help find the airstrip on his next venture. Asking King about the airstrip would be easier but for now he'll keep this to himself. A broad smile emerges as he leans back in his chair with his hands locked behind his neck. Having knowledge about something special on the ranch boosts his spirits.

Brett may be Gabby's perfect cowboy but I have useful skills as well. But that raises a profound question, why am I still competing? Even though they're married, I'll show her that she made the wrong choice. She should have picked me.

Fifteen years ago, when Stan was in college, he took instructions and obtained a single engine private pilot's license. The license is no longer current, but he could have it reinstated with the mandatory three take-offs and landings. Having his pilot's license would be fun and time-efficient as he could fly back and forth from DC right to the ranch instead of flying into the county airport, which is a two-hour drive away. If he decides to go back home ... and that is still a decision he needs to make.

He hasn't made any plans for his future but the conversation with Rusty and Jamie has brought the subject forefront. Should he stay here in Texas and continue helping with the ranch and doing the accounting and scheduling at the EAT Program or should he return to the East Coast? His mother has pleaded with him to stay, and she'd be disappointed with his decision to leave, but given time she would understand if he showed her that it would make him happy. However, first, he needs to answer a very important question—apart from having Gabby, and that isn't very likely to happen now that she's married—what else would make him happy?

In the past, spending time outdoors always removed the fog in his mind when he was in a place of indecision, and it may work again this time. He'll plan a camping trip to check out the location of the airstrip. He'll tell King and Rusty that he's inspecting the perimeter fences and structures such as the old windmill and the ground wells scattered throughout. He'll say he's surveying the land to see if it would be feasible to invest in a solar farm so that the ranch could be self-sufficient as well as provide energy for others. He'll also check out cell phone coverage and note areas of no or weakened signals.

He'll pick a time when the forecast is favorable for a spectacular view of the Milky Way. Without any ambient light on the far corners of the ranch, the big Texas sky will be amazingly beautiful. He can try out his new Celestron telescope and really get a great view of the universe. He'll take some great photos with the camera. According to the literature, he'll be able to take pictures of the rings around Saturn. He can't get that back in DC, but his main goal will be to find that airstrip.

As a teenager he was an Eagle Scout, so he's had experience in the outdoors. He'll gather his ten essentials and other provisions to last a few days. This far south, February is a good month to camp as the nights are still cool enough for a sleeping bag and daytime won't leave him baking in the hot sun. He's certain that this trip will be just what he needs. During his next session, he'll run the plan by his shrink, just so all of his bases are covered. An unexcused absence would set him back a few months and he doesn't wish for that.

He turns away from the desk to see Ryder still asleep on his bed. Ryder will be the perfect companion on this mission. His breed is known for having high energy and a protective temperament. Since Stan brought him home, he's gained fifteen pounds and is twice as strong. When Stan wrestles with him and when they tussle with the pull toy, it quickly becomes obvious that Ryder is thriving. He's proved repeatedly that he is a good watchdog and that will be helpful. There have been recent reports of illegal immigrants passing through after crossing the Mexican border.

Stan has no desire to see anyone or cause anyone trouble, but he's well aware that when folks are running scared, tired and hungry, the dark adds another uncertainty, and anything is possible. He's seen the news reports, and having Ryder at his side will definitely be an asset.

Glancing at his clock, it's almost 2 a.m. As if the power of suggestion takes hold he stretches, then yawns. Morning will be here before he's ready. He'd better try once more to get some shuteye before the sun breaks the horizon line.

CHAPTER 7

Stan wakes up to a wet face and doggie breath. Pushing Ryder away he groans and checks the time. It's after 7 a.m.; he forgot to set his alarm.

"I'm so late." He pets the dog then buries under the cover. Ryder thinks it's a game and pounces on him pulling the blanket away with his mouth.

"Okay, okay, I'm up." Stan throws the covers off, dons the jeans thrown over the back of the chair and grabs a clean t-shirt. He catches his profile in the mirror; like Ryder, he's also gaining weight but it's fat, not muscle. These months of recuperating from his motorcycle accident have kept him from a strict workout schedule. He needs to work on his fitness.

Seconds later, they exit the room side by side, but Ryder is quick to push in front as they head down the stairs.

"I know, you're in a hurry to go out. I'm doing the best I can." He forgot his cane so he hobbles, taking one step at a time. He opens the door and before he turns his head, Ryder's gone. "Don't run off," he yells.

He ambles to the kitchen where Jamie always has a pot of fresh-ly brewed coffee. Rita bought a Keurig, but Rusty and Jamie prefer coffee brewed the old-fashioned way, and Stan agrees that not only is the taste better, but the smell is incredible. He reaches for his ther-mos, a gift from his stint in rehab. It's a reminder each morning to say three things for which he is grateful. During rehab classes he was taught that research shows grateful people are less apt to be depressed. He's hopeful that following the steps given will keep him from the downward spiral of depression and addiction that landed him flat on his ass, not a situation to repeat.

His nose sniffs out the cinnamon-apple coffee cake sitting on the counter. Several slices are missing so he knows the others are finished with breakfast, reinforcing the obvious—he's late. He touch-es the cake and it's still warm, so where is Jamie? He leans over the sink to get a better view out of the window and sees Jamie and Rusty playing fetch with Ryder. They love that dog as much as he does, and he's grateful since Ryder requires more exercise than Stan can cur-rently give. With his injured leg, it takes him a while to get moving so it would be a hardship first thing in the morning to play a game of catch with his adopted friend. He makes a mental note: That's one gratefulness, he needs two more to complete his assignment. The corners of his mouth turn upward as he pops a piece of the coffee cake into his mouth, washing it down with the black coffee. This morning his situation doesn't seem as daunting. Was he overreacting yesterday?

It's a sunny day and he's eating a homemade delight and drinking a coffee that's on par with Starbucks. Yes, cake and coffee, that would be gratefulness number two. Plus, he's smiling. A good attitude proves extremely important so that makes gratefulness number three. Mission accomplished.

His improved mood is short-lived as the honking of a car horn gets his attention, followed seconds later by voices and laughter. Curious, he returns to the kitchen window. Seeing Brett throwing the ball for Ryder to catch triggers the green monster to grip Stan's soul. *Ryder is my dog. If Brett wants to play catch, he needs to get his own dog.* Jamie's advice mills around in his brain. Perhaps she is right. Will he ever find happiness here in Texas with Brett and Gabby front-and-center in his life?

The front door swings open and Gabby enters. Her blond strands are back in a ponytail and her stretch jeans fit tight revealing her curves. Any warm-blooded male would notice.

"Morning, Stan. You want to catch a ride with us to work?" *She's always so cheerful.*

"Sorry, I'm running a bit late." He shrugs. "I'll drive on my own."

"We can wait. There're no appointments this morning so it doesn't matter if we get there late. Besides Brett's having a good time with Ryder. The exercise is good for them both."

"No, you go on. I just got up. Couldn't sleep." He rubs his forehead.

"Is your leg bothering you?" She has that "poor baby" tone in her voice that makes him want to erupt like a volcano and spew her pity back at her. But he pinches his mouth tight and smiles.

"Nope, it wasn't the leg." He continues to force the smile. "I'll see you later." He raises his mug up in the air as if shooing her out of the door. He turns his back and holds his breath.

He listens for the sound of the porch door closing and is thankful that she left. He's aware that she means well, but mentioning his leg repeatedly is annoying. He wants to be normal. He's not handicapped; he has a slight limp. He's not mentally challenged; many people see psychiatrists. He made a mistake but with correction it has given him some grit. When will people stop coddling him like he's a fragile piece of glass ready to shatter? Will Gabby ever see him as the man he is?

CHAPTER 8

At the Equine Center

A few days later in his office, with his appointment calendar clear, Stan gets his treasured map from his leather portfolio, unfolds the torn, yellowed document and spreads it on his desk. He's as giddy as a kid with a new toy. With calipers in hand he remeasures the distances between the landmarks, marking down his findings on another paper. Is this map drawn to scale? It doesn't have a legend. He won't know until he sets out on his journey, uncertain. He's deep in concentration.

Gabby stands in the door frame. "Hey," she says quietly as if not to disturb Ryder. "You okay?"

He hides the document with the appointment calendar. "Why do you ask?" He bites on the end of his pen.

"I don't know. You seem quiet...preoccupied." Her hands leave her hips; she scans his face and leans over his desk as if demanding an answer.

Uncomfortable with the small distance between them, Stan slides his chair back and interlocks his fingers, placing his hands behind his neck. "I'm usually quiet." Her scent makes his brain reel. *I'll play this game. Can she see my heart beats faster when she's near?*

"This is different ...like you're preoccupied. Your visits with Doctor Dan going well?"

"Couldn't be better."

"Are you upset with me?"

"No." He raises his eyebrows and fakes a smile. "Did you do something?"

She avoids answering and rolls her eyes. "Are you upset with Brett?"

"No. Really, Gabby, this line of questioning is ridiculous."

"Sorry, I'm just concerned. That's all."

She stands there another few seconds as if waiting for him to offer an explanation. Remaining tight-lipped, he doesn't budge so she turns and leaves. Unaware that he had been holding his breath, he lets it out slowly, shakes his head, then searches upward as if thanking God for the end to her interrogation. He rubs his brow and hangs his head.

Their conversation, though brief, was enough of a distraction that he's unable to concentrate. What if she comes back? Gingerly, he folds the map and tucks it away. It's been slow here today, and after two earlier appointments the schedule is clear. He can slip out. One of the volunteer veterans is working, cleaning out stalls and tending to the horses, so that's not a concern, and Gabby has been known to answer the phone if it rings repeatedly, thinking that he momentarily stepped away from his desk. He'll saddle up Sadie and take pleasure in this sunny day. Enjoying nature always lifts his spirit and after his encounter with Gabby, he needs a little pick-me-up. A change in scenery should improve his funky mood.

Riding Sadie proves beneficial. His mood's lighter and he's improved his right leg as riding strengthens leg muscles. Another benefit to horseback riding is that it provides a sense of control, and control is power. This afternoon after Gabby's visit, he needed to regain control. Before his accident, he never thought much about power; he never had to. He lived life on his own terms but after the accident that all changed. When one loses control over the physical body, the mind suffers as well, he learned.

Returning to the center, he follows the path into the corral and sucks in his breath as his newfound positive spirit evaporates at the sight of Gabby walking toward him fast, as if there is urgency. Dismounting, he grunts as he bears weight on his left leg. Better to do this before she reads the pain on his face. Another "poor baby" look may ignite his internal dynamite.

"So that's why you disappeared. You could have told me. I took Ryder looking for you." She shields her eyes from the sun. "Hey, Brett's here, I'm leaving. Are you going home soon?"

"I need to brush down Sadie and feed her. Then I'll call it a day."

"You'll be okay, right?" Even with her hand shielding her face, the brightness makes her squint. "Are you coming home for dinner or are you going off by yourself again?" Biting her lip, her tone is sharp. "You're acting weird."

He avoids her stare. "You needn't be concerned. I'm fine." He uses a hitch knot to secure Sadie to the fence and starts to unbuckle the saddle.

"I'm your friend. You can tell me anything. Really, if something is bothering you..." Her eyes are pleading. "We used to be close." She pouts.

Nervous, he laughs aloud. *Can she be so naïve?*

"What's so funny?"

"Gabby, that was before..."

"Before what?"

Is she really asking that? They have a history. Just short of nine months ago, he had asked her to marry him and he offered to be a father to her unborn child. He thought her smarter. *Okay, I'm tired of this game. Better to get it out in the open.* "Before you and Brett got married. You made a choice. Now I'm trying to respect your choice."

She opens her mouth as if to say something.

He hangs the saddle in the barn. "I can't be close to you. I'm doing my best to make an impossible situation tolerable. Respectfully, it would be great if you would do the same."

Her brow is furled, her eyes wide as if in disbelief. Thick lashes fight back her tears.

"I thought we were past that."

"It doesn't work that way. I can't turn off how I feel. I thought you understood."

His eyes scan her face. Wet tracks run down her cheeks. Seeing any grown woman cry raises his need to comfort, and to have this particular woman cry—God, his comfort needle is off the chart. Throwing off all ordinary judgment, he rushes to her side, pulling her into his arms. He's doing everything that he vowed never to do. He strokes her smooth hair, feels her warmth and smells her scent. He's tired of skating around the truth, pretending that he doesn't care. This gesture has broken every rule.

"I need you to be happy. But seeing you with him is a nightmare for me. Can you understand that? It's not just the leg, Gabby, it's my heart that's broken. That's what landed me in rehab. It was easier to drink and take drugs than to face rejection and watch the two of you together. Now, I'm working hard to find a new path. I was hoping that time would heal. It's taking longer than I thought and it's harder than I thought. I'm trying my best." His deep sigh matches the big burden he disclosed.

He pauses to collect his thoughts, stepping into dangerous territory. "We're family; it's tough, really tough. I'm doing my best. Mother loves having me around and asked me to stay. It was an easy choice. I love horses and getting this new business off the ground. And riding for my own therapy has been awesome. You started all of this for me and I am grateful." He searches her eyes and wipes the wetness from her cheek. "Still, I need to figure it all out. This is your home. Maybe I should go back East and rebuild my life there."

He caves to temptation and pulls her in tight once again. His hands needing more, he rubs her back. Even though in pain, he is in heaven. "It would put some distance between us." His words voice the opposite of his heart. *I'm a pathetic hypocrite.* "Maybe Eric and Andrew will hire me at their EAT program in Virginia." He can't help but smile when he hears her sniffles. "Oh, my sweet girl, I don't want to ever make you sad."

He's intoxicated by her warmth and scent. It's driving him insane. However, the noise of the door opening across the corral, at the main building, breaks the moment and warns him to stop holding her.

Facing them, Brett stands with his arms crossed. He yells, "Gabby, I've been waiting."
Startled, she pulls away, but neither utters a word, which seems to spark Brett's curiosity.

"Is something wrong?"

"Nothing's wrong. Stan just brought Sadie back." Gabby waves at Brett and forces a smile, then turns to wipe her face with the sleeve of her shirt.

She lifts her head to meet his eyes. "Guess I'd better go. I'll see you later at the house." She turns away. "I'm sorry."

She runs through the door that Brett holds open.

"What was that all about? It looked serious." He searches her eyes for an answer; her red eyes and nose are a telltale sign that she has been crying. "What did he say to you?" His eyes scan her face. "I'll take care of him." His tone is harsh as he abruptly opens the door wider to push by her.

She pulls on his arm in an effort to stop him. "Brett, please don't... it's nothing."

"You're crying, that's something. I'm tired of him upsetting you."

"He's not upsetting me. I was helping him. He's depressed." She pinches her lip. "I'd feel awful if he went back to using drugs."

"Stan is not your responsibility. You can't fix him. If you're that concerned, you need to get your dad and Rita involved."

"You don't understand. It's not like that. He's trying to cope.

Okay, he went riding. That's good for him both physically and mentally. He's doing the right things."

"Then why are you so upset? It has to be more than that."

"It's hard for him. He's dealing with it. Brett, let's just go. Okay, come on, please." Brett rolls his eyes but complies.

Leaving the center, they are silent and avoid touching as they walk to the red convertible. Brett lets out a deep sigh as he opens the door and starts the engine. "I know you don't want to hear this but I'm going to say it anyway." He pats her hand. "Stan uses his disability to gain your sympathy. I'm sorry, but a guy doesn't put his arms around another man's wife." His voice gains strength. "Okay. He's crossing boundaries. Do you hear me? I can't allow that. I will not be made to look like a fool. It needs to stop—and now."

She buckles her seatbelt. "He's not just a guy, he's family. There's a difference."

"Oh, princess. Not this time. That argument doesn't work here." He's seen that facial expression before; she's upset. "Look, I'm sorry if I sound harsh, but put yourself in my shoes."

"You need to trust me. Can you do that?" She rubs his upper arm and sticks out her lower lip. The gesture works as his half-smile provokes one on her.

"I know that you make it a mission to save every one of God's creatures. It's one of the things that make you you, and I love that. But you cannot save Stan."

She places her arm around his neck. "I hate when we fight. I love you, Brett. I was just trying to help him. I'm sorry if I upset you but it's nice that you get jealous." She wraps her finger around a curl of his hair and whispers a promise in his ear. He giggles and she smiles.

Thank God, that was easy, she thinks. All's forgotten as they pass through the gate with the wind blowing their hair.

Back at the Equine Center, Stan feeds Sadie and fills a bowl of water for Ryder. He doublechecks all the gates and doors. Checking his cell, he knows he's late for dinner, but he's allowing time for Brett and Gabby to arrive at the ranch first.

He recalls that tonight's meal is a gift from Jamie as she's preparing all of his favorites. Yes, yesterday it was Jamie, now today it's Gabby. Seems like everyone detects his misery. That camping trip providing several days away from all of this chaos is the best idea that he's entertained in a while. He dials Doctor Dan's office. They're closed but he leaves a message.

He grabs his leather pouch with his secret treasure map and his cane before turning off the lights. Ryder barks as if telling him to get the move on. "Yes, boss, ten-four. You're the best, you know that?" He leans over, allowing Ryder to lick his face. "I love you too. Let's go, we don't want to be late for dinner."

CHAPTER 9

"Jamie, you outdid yourself. It's gonna take a bulldozer to get me out of this chair." Stan rubs his stomach. Everyone laughs. Unlike last evening's dinner, there's a full table tonight for the pot roast dinner. His mother and King came back a day early. It isn't unusual for them to change plans on the spur of the moment.

King is a genuine Texas rancher, hard-working, a devout Christian, and greatly respected by everyone who knows him. Over the decades as his oil wells generated more revenue than the cattle, he has become more involved in the political scene as he continues to buy land, organize the ranchers and lobby congressmen. Most think he should run for governor.

As these duties have taken him away from the ranch, he's promoted Rusty to foreman, in charge of the day-to-day workings of the ranch. The three-hundred-thousand-acre ranch is a lot of real estate, much more land than one man to handle. After Gabby's mother died a few years ago, King pulled Rusty and Jamie closer into his circle and invited them to live in the main house.

While it is Rusty's job to take care of the cattle, King controls the business end, which involves maintaining close contact with the politicians, so he purchased a condo in the city. He could wine and dine them after office hours and then he'd retreat to his condo. It will be a year this April that King and Rita married. Rita enjoys the city life as much as King enjoys the country. As long as she owns and manages her art gallery, King has agreed to spend more time in the city. Marriage is always a compromise.

"I'm glad you enjoyed it. It's wonderful to have a full table," Jamie says as she starts to clear the table of dishes.

"I'd rather be here than in the city any day," Kings says. "The food's better." He chuckles.

"But it's wonderful to dine in a fancy restaurant and shop. I got some real bargains downtown. Most stores had a sale," says Rita.

"With work at the gallery, when did you find time to shop?" He leans over and kisses her on her cheek.

"A woman can always find time to shop, dear." Laughter flows around the table.

King drains the last of his wine. "While you were at ArtSmart, I saw Richard. When I first called his office, his secretary said I should call back in a few days. Then I reminded her that Richard was in that office because of me—my efforts and my money."

"Later when I met with that pompous lawyer face-to-face, I said, 'You're a senator, not God.' I hope our little conversation pulled him out of the clouds. His feet better hit the ground running and start the work he was hired to do. Our bill comes out of committee soon and we don't have enough votes for it to pass. So disappointing but not a surprise." King rubs his chin.

Brett looks to Gabby with raised eyebrows and she bites her tongue. She and Richard were engaged before she dated Brett, and his look seems to say, *How were you ever involved with that asshole?* She smiles, with her eyes saying, *I married you, not him.*

King sits forward and puts his elbows on the table. "I would be delighted if you'll all put Friday, two weeks from today, on your calendar. Rita's bringing a renowned artist—by the way, a friend of the president of this here United States—to showcase his work at ArtSmart and she'll need help with the opening. I've invited every statesmen and oilman in Texas." He turns to his wife. "What's your fire code limit, Rita?"

He squeezes her hand, then gives a hearty chuckle. "It will be a busy evening; first on the agenda, dinner at the country club, next we'll move to ArtSmart for coffee and dessert." He switches his gaze toward Gabby. "I know you're busy with the equine center, but if you could help Rita, I'm sure she'd appreciate any time you can give her. You too, Stan."

People respond positively to King; it's the reason he's successful. Excitement brews around the table.

"Sure, Daddy, I would love to help. Sounds exciting," Gabby says. "Amanda could help too. That is, if Richard and she are still a couple."

"I believe they are. That's a great idea. I'll make it a point to talk with her. Behind every man is a good woman, and she impresses me as someone who can keep Richard on track. Thanks for the tip."

Rita turns to Gabby and says, "On that same subject, you may want to update your wall at the gallery with some of your new paintings. Your new contemporary pieces will complement his work and there'll be buyers in the crowd."

All this talk about art has caught her by surprise. Gabby's situation proves to be just the opposite of her daddy's as lately she spends all of her time at the ranch. In her late twenties, after returning from an unsuccessful two years trying to make it big as an artist in New York City, she worked full-time in Rita's gallery and visited the ranch on an occasional weekend. Her art career has taken a definite back seat with her focus on the Equine Center. Her daddy warned her that this would be the case when he handed her the investment check for the one million dollars that she requested, but she was determined to open the center, a decision she doesn't regret.

Now since marrying Brett, she finished building their house at the ranch, started working at the Equine Center, and works an occasional shift at ArtSmart, but only if Rita's desperate for the help. Having a studio in her house has made it easy to paint and she's giving her work new direction with a different style.

"Stan, if you could be your mother's assistant that would help. The center will have to survive for a few days without you." King must have heard Stan gasp. Gabby and Stan share a look of concern.

"I wouldn't ask if this wasn't critical. You both know that, right? I understand your work's important, but this takes priority. It's missions like this that provided the gift money to make the center a reality. It'll only be for two weeks. Can I count on you?"

"Daddy, maybe Stan and Brett could collaborate," Gabby says. "Surely, for something this crucial, Rusty can spare Brett a day or two. Some of our clients at the center have scheduling needs involving transportation, since the center's far from town. Someone needs to coordinate their appointments and rides. It would be a hardship for them if both Stan and I weren't there." She looks to Brett.

"If I'm going to showcase my new series at the gallery, I'll need help with the installation. Brett and I haven't been to the city since that New Year's party last month. We'll look at coordinating our schedules. I'll make sure everything's covered. Promise."

King nods his head in approval. "Work with Rita. I'm leavin' all the details up to her. Okay, that settles it. A family working together. I like that a lot. Let's toast to a successful event." Realizing that his wine glass is empty, King holds up his water glass instead as he leans back in his chair sporting a wide grin.

CHAPTER 10

At the King Ranch

Stan shifts his weight, leaning his elbow on the bathroom counter giving him a better view of the tattoo on his left shoulder. He nods his head and grins. It's the first time he's been able to admire this tribute to his star-gazing mentor. The mirror clouds with steam again; now his cherished star resembles a blue blob, not nearly as impressive. He wipes the mirror again.

It's been twenty-four hours, so he's allowed to keep the tattoo unbandaged, but he won't show it to anyone. His secret evokes a chuckle, an escape of bittersweet emotion. Having secrets makes him feel special; however, from his tainted past, too many secrets have proved destructive. He's treading on dangerous ground.

The rain continues to pound on the metal roof of the ranch house. He's been restless since the daily bouts of rain postponed his camping trip. His pent-up anxiety contributed to his bad habit of picking his cuticles until they bled, prompting the need to inflict pain in a more acceptable fashion—hence the tattoo. The impulsive decision proved beneficial, as the endorphins temporarily released his lovesick soul from its prison. *Gabby, I should forget you, but I won't. This star, I'll always treasure and there's nothing anyone can do to take that away.*

In the great room an hour later sipping an early dinner martini, his pacing halts as an unfamiliar photo frame begs his attention. This new addition must be a purchase from his mother's recent boasted shopping spree. He holds the frame at eye level, minimizing the glare. Beaming back is a photo of Brett decked out in his cowboy attire with one arm around Gabby's waist while she holds a large silver belt buckle. Tapping on the frame, he bites his lip and closes his eyes as he recalls that day at the National Finals Rodeo. It was this past December in Las Vegas.

"Brett, Brett, this is wonderful." Gabby's joyful voice echoed, an irresistible sound for Stan to follow as he limped slowly toward the stage—just in time to see her wrap her arms around Brett's neck, followed by a huge kiss.

Stan felt his pulse quicken and his anger level rose as King followed in congratulating Brett. He had patted him on the back, wearing a smile that illuminated his entire face as a sunbeam might. Brett gleamed back proudly before presenting the belt to King, the prize for coming in second in the national calf-roping event. The photo session seemed endless with photographers from the newspapers and trending magazines. Reporters accompanied by their film teams took turns getting footage for television stations. Stan thought the fanfare would never end.

Then a few days later, the celebration continued at the ranch when King threw another party, inviting the wranglers and neighbors from the entire county. All the excitement proved a nauseating experience.

A bitter taste forms in Stan's mouth. He remembers it all too well. Yes, it was another highlight for Brett that reinforced Stan's inferiority complex, especially where Gabby was involved. *Why do women fall for that stuff?* He rolls his eyes and takes another sip of his martini. *A framed photo today and what next...a life-sized portrait over the mantel?* Disgusting. He rubs his forehead.

If this continues, he may go camping, even with the rain. He lifts the curtains to peer outside. No rain at present...a good sign. He's obtained approval from his doctor and his supplies are packed. If Mother Nature had cooperated, he'd be away from all of this and finding that airstrip. He kneads his thigh, convincing himself that it's this dampness making his bones ache.

He checks his cell phone for the latest weather report. The forecast is sure to improve; this is Texas, not Seattle. However, there is one benefit to the rainy days. They reduce the appointments at the Equine Center and, by switching the calls over to his cell, it allows him to assist his mother with preparations for King's upcoming important event. At least his mother is happy with his efforts. Regardless, he could care less. Out of boredom, he lifts the curtain once more, but the only change is the dimming light as day made way for night. Where is everyone?

PART II

CHAPTER 11

Beyond the Eastern Border of the King Ranch

Human trafficking provides the labor for both the marijuana farm and the sex slave business. After being kidnapped or willfully accepting an empty promise that would lead to a better life, the victims, which include women and teenagers, both boys and girls, are blindfolded, beaten or drugged before being transported to a remote location, a place far off the grid. Hidden from law enforcement and relatives, they are prisoners with guards on duty, twenty-four/seven. They sleep in overcrowded bunkhouses and are given minimal food and water. They are dehumanized, treated as items to be worked, traded or sold.

At this location, in the barren Texas countryside is the farm where they work cultivating, harvesting and processing the marijuana.

Once every few weeks, the noise from the motors of the all-terrain vehicles can be heard before being seen as they navigate the rough landscape toward the compound. They come dropping off supplies and reloading with the precious commodity. There are orders for both the marijuana product and the sex business. Turnover of both victims and employees is high. In this business, there are no guarantees and many simply vanish. No questions asked.

Frequently the victims chosen to work the farm will be weakened from the lack of food, poor living conditions, and even a continued high. Proving unproductive, they'll be transferred to the sex trafficking side of the business.

Knowing the privileges may include hot showers, better meals and clean clothes, in the camp a transfer to the sex business is horrifically glorified. With rumors of a wealthy client base, stories circulate about victims sold who got lucky and lived the life of a modern-day Cinderella. These fairytales concocted by the guards create a cruel fantasy, so the victims view it as their best avenue for escape; perhaps these tales help prisoners struggling to make it through the day to avoid thoughts about their unfortunate lot in life.

There isn't much revenue for the cartel in marketing only marijuana. However, lacing the dried leaves with a product such as phencyclidine (PCP), known on the streets as angel dust, the cannabis is advertised as "enhanced." This not only brings a better price for a bolder high, but is more addictive to ensure that the buyer would become a long-term client, open to buying more expensive products in the future. These enhanced products on the street, known as fry, or superweed, make the farm a lucrative investment.

To ensure order, keeping his employees loyal, the boss makes unscheduled appearances. All the victims are gathered and ordered to stand at attention. At times, the boss searches for a specific victim, other times he can be influenced by the guards as to uncooperative workers, and sometimes, a victim is chosen just because the boss wishes.

Around the farm, creative ways have been invented by the forced laborers to smuggle and enjoy the marijuana. The guards usually turn a blind eye and quite frankly don't care. If high, the victims are less likely to escape and if they do try, their impaired judgment will cause their downfall. And if caught, punishment can mean death. Sometimes it is necessary to make an ugly and unforgettable example out of the potential escapee to help keep the others terrified for their lives. It is a horrifying existence for the victims and in most instances life-threatening. For those in charge it is equally as dangerous, but it is also a very profitable business. The higher the stakes, the higher the profit. Those who don't have much to lose consider it a game...a dangerous game.

There is no end to the creativity that flows around the farm when it comes to smoking weed. For example, when in need of papers to roll reefers, the girls save wrappers from tampons distributed for their monthly periods. They're also alert for discarded cigarette butts to light their carefully rolled joints or they bum cigarettes from the guards with the promise of a favor. In addition, the women assigned to kitchen duties steal potatoes and apples, as these can be hollowed out and used as pipes. Pipes can also be made from empty toilet paper rolls wrapped in smuggled aluminum foil. The guards tend to roll their eyes and find it comical as to the lengths the prisoners will go for some weed. But the drug dulls this existence and provides a brief escape.

Marie Gomez had worked the farm for only a week. One of the guards took a liking to her and she played along, obtaining information. She seldom spoke but listened carefully. When the time was right, the moon not too bright, with few guards on duty, she would make a run. She had a plan. She refused to live this way.

CHAPTER 12

S tan surveys the landscape, searching the horizon as beads of sweat trickle down his temples. Brushing them away with a quick swipe, he retrieves the binoculars from the passenger seat of the Jeep. Investigating the rocky incline to the left, his eyes open wider, accompanied by a slight upward curve of his lip. His suspicions are correct as the western ridge that supposedly borders the abandoned airstrip, the goal of this trip, is in sight.

A glance at the sun's distance above the horizon confirms the hour and he checks his watch for verification. His guess would have been ten minutes off the actual time but he's pleased for this accuracy of his growing knowledge base. This cowboy stuff could actually be his thing. He's visiting new territory as he passed the last fenced pasture on the King property at least eight miles ago. The vastness of the King ranch is certainly mindboggling. Relaxing his shoulders, he takes in a deep breath, aware of the slight drop in temperature and limited daylight remaining. It was forecasted to be a cool, clear February evening. He'll need to set up camp soon.

First, he whistles for Ryder. The dog had gone off exploring as soon as the Jeep stopped. He's probably sniffing every rock and prickly pear cactus, hoping to scare out rabbits and prairie dogs. Stan's certain that Ryder hasn't been successful in finding any critters because he hasn't heard barking, as Ryder's proud to inform him of his finds. Once he found a rattlesnake and by the grace of God, he wasn't bitten. Stan hates snakes. He listens again before calling. *Where is that dog?* He thinks he's using the proper whistle that Rusty had said was the come-back command. Ryder isn't obeying.

Filling his lungs with air and rolling back his shoulders once again, he's thankful for this chance to escape family and have alone time, enjoying these open spaces. Taking this moment to check in with himself, a tool used to determine his mental status, he decides this trip is proving to be a good decision. It's surprising this sense of clarity he's experiencing after six months of ambiguity and indecision.

Then just when he thinks he's safe, the obvious reason for his dilemma resurfaces. *Gabby, Gabby, Gabby...*damn...she's always there in his mind, invading his thoughts. *But Gabby chose Brett. Let her go.*

His mind tells his heart this repeatedly; however, his heart carries this love. Does anyone ever forget their first love? That undeniable love that shines like a star, igniting a warmth that pervades all—body, mind, and spirit. With rejection, that warmth has turned into a flame that burnt, leaving scars. The pain of it all is still exists but his therapist assures him that time can heal. He's still waiting.

He really doesn't wish to let her go. He cherishes the nights she visits his dreams; there she's so close. He can smell her hair and see the sparkle in her eyes. He yearns to touch her, but in every dream, the harder he tries to reach for her, the farther away she drifts. He always awakens abruptly, discouraged, and it feels as though he's never slept at all. It's an endless cycle that is both mentally and physically exhausting. Their close encounter, having her in his arms this past week at the Equine Center, flamed that inner spark giving it new life, restarting the relentless cycle.

As if on cue his leg starts to ache. He rubs it vigorously before sliding behind the wheel of the Jeep. Calling for Ryder hasn't produced the mutt but he's sure this will. Turning over the engine, he revs the motor. Within seconds, a figure emerges from the thicket and Ryder's running full force toward him.

"Get in, Boss. Where have you been?"

With one giant leap, he bounds off the running board and lands in the Jeep. Stan pulls a few briars from the dog's ears. "You've been busy. It shows."

Ryder barks and it seems as though he's smiling.

Stan's foot hits the gas pedal hard as he steers sharply to the left The tires skid as the dirt and gravel flies, creating a cloud. With his right arm he steadies Ryder to prevent him from lurching into the dash.

Precious daylight moments are dwindling. After a few minutes, the Jeep comes to a stop near a small grove of sagebrush close to the ridge. This is the perfect place to set up camp and end the day.

Grabbing a few more logs from the back of the Jeep, he places two on the fire. This is his favorite time of the day—his belly full from a meal of beef kabobs and a baked potato, a cold beer in his hand, the soft sounds of a slow, crackling fire, as he's propped up in his sleeping bag with Ryder at his side. A cool breeze roams through the otherwise still night. He's elected to bed down under the stars, forgoing his tent, as the cares of the world seem far away in this magical setting with the stars as his ceiling.

With his eyes focusing heavenward, he's able to follow the trail of the Milky Way across the galaxy. The stars...so beautiful...then the stars remind him of his tattoo and a mere leap, once more to Gabby. She's everywhere, even here. The pain in his leg stirs.

Stan needs to use another mindful exercise that he learned in rehab—when something unpleasant fills your thoughts, counteract that with a positive thought to give a proper perspective, stopping the negative downward spiral. This technique reminds him that aside from losing the love battle for Gabby, there are other areas in his life these past years that have been pretty darn good. His motorcycle accident could have left him in a wheelchair—or even dead. But he's alive and walking and here on this picture-perfect night. He's financially secure for life, another one of his secrets.

In his past when he worked as an attorney in DC, he met a brilliant young lawyer who proposed a far-fetched scheme to invest in his startup software company. Stan, of course, was skeptical but appreciated the enthusiasm of his friend and invested. Over the next several years, his friend left the law firm and their friendship waned. Stan had written the money off as a loss. But three years later, the friend came to the law office with a handshake and a wide grin. His company made it big, and the check for Stan was a hundredfold the original amount invested, with more promised in the future. The friend thanked Stan repeatedly for having faith in him and his company all those years ago.

Although Stan has never breathed a word of this to his family, he's certain that the rich and influential Wayne King must have hired detectives to scope out the Adams family before proposing marriage to Rita. If indeed King does know, he's honored Stan's secret because his mother seems to be clueless.

The mindfulness exercise worked as these positive thoughts have stopped the negative spiral and he's less focused on the pain. It restores his faith in therapy since many times he's left the sessions thinking it was all a waste. In this peaceful state, a well-deserved sleep overtakes him.

CHAPTER 13

Ryder still nests snuggled close and Stan feels the chill in the early morning air on his face.

"Wake up, Boss," he says in a loud whisper. "Time to start our day." The dog lifts his head but then returns to his sleeping position.

"If you want breakfast, you'll need to scoot over a bit as I can't unzip this bag with you there." He pushes him gently but Ryder remains in place. Stan pets his head and Ryder yawns before licking Stan's hand. His tongue is rough and it tickles.

"You wore yourself out with all that exploring yesterday. You rest but I need to get moving." After crawling out of the sleeping bag, he uses his hands to push off the ground so he can stand. "Damn," he mutters for his leg is stiff and currently refuses to bend at the knee and he has no feeling in his foot. He rubs it before searching for his cane.

Checking the level of the sun above the horizon, he forgoes cooking over the fire as it had gone out over the night. Sure, some embers may lurk beneath but it would take more work to stoke than he wants to invest. His white gas stove will suffice to heat enough water for coffee and oatmeal. It will be a quick breakfast as he's excited to drive to the airstrip and get footage with his drone. After fixing his meal, he pours the leftover water into Ryder's bowl and mixes a concoction with the dry food pellets. The sounds and smells of meal preparation have Ryder standing ready before Stan has a chance to place the bowl on the ground.

"I knew food would get you moving."

Taking sips of his last ounces of coffee, Stan unfolds the yellowed map to refresh his memory before placing it into the inside pocket of his backpack.

Breaking camp, he steers south in hopes of finding a path to get into the plateau where the airstrip should be located. Driving in this direction for several miles proves correct as there is a narrow path, perhaps made by a herd of wild horses, that seems smooth enough for the Jeep to pass. His quiet-spoken "Thank God" reminds him of his daily habit of gratefulness: one, he's thankful for the path; two, he's thankful for the clear skies and the warmth of the sun; three, he'll offer up thanks in advance for finding the airstrip. Satisfied with the completion of his assignment, he reaches across to pet Ryder.

"Nothing against having more than three. I'm grateful that you're here," he says to his companion who gives him daily unconditional love. "You're a good pal. Ready for another day of adventure?"

Ryder barks as if on cue and Stan smiles, almost certain that the mutt understands.

Even though the path looked smooth, it turned out to have some significant ruts. Twice the Jeep was hung up on two wheels and repeated forward and reverse motion got it moving again. Then he had to backtrack in reverse a few hundred feet and take an alternative route. After the sun was high in the sky, the landscape leveled.

Anxious to fly the drone, Stan hurries to get the quadcopter ready for its flight. He wipes his forehead with his red handkerchief when a bead of sweat drops on the screen. He isn't prepared for this intense heat wave, especially in February.

The drone flies steady as the air is still. He can get a full ten miles in diameter but that's not necessary. From a first quick look at the video, it seems the map was correct. The runway is less than a half-mile away. He's excited but he'll eat lunch before heading off. Driving the perimeter of the airstrip and documenting with the drone will take him a full hour or more, and he's starved now. His pulse speeds and he pumps his fist.

He retrieves a brisket sandwich from the cooler and dumps almost a third of the bottle of barbecue sauce on it. Accompanying his sandwich is a large dill pickle and potato chips. When he "camps" he wants to enjoy life, and mealtimes are usually the highlight of the day. He opens a can of flavored sparkling water to break the monotony of drinking water from his Kangaroo. He checks the footage that the drone captured on its first pass-through. Stan sits more erect in his chair, squints, and then zooms in for a better view.

"Well, I'll be damned." He looks around for Ryder, who is nowhere in sight, as if the dog would understand about his find.

Stan turns his attention back to the screen. It seems that on the airstrip there are wheel tracks on the ground, molded from the past rain. The tracks seem to be different wheel-width sizes, so there must be tracks from other vehicles than just a plane. If he's correct, this landing strip has been used recently—as well as the surrounding land. But who did it and why are the two questions that immediately pop into his mind. He's certain that he's still on King's property; however, there aren't any oil derricks this far south so that eliminates the possibility that the tracks are from the transport of the oil.

Hurrying to clean up so he can get a closer look at that airstrip and those tire marks, he tries hard to figure things out. He knows King's whereabouts these past ten days, and most of his business has taken him into town as he prepares for the famous visiting artist, Templeton.

Suddenly he hears Ryder in the distance. Familiar with Ryder's daily tones, he realizes this bark is different. It barks urgency. Stan's reminded of their run-in with the rattlesnake and shakes his head. With haste, he grabs the shovel to use as a cane, believing it may come in handy if a snake is the cause for the ruckus.

He limps in the direction of the sound. "Ryder, what did you find?" The barking continues. The trek longer and more arduous than he anticipated, Stan hobbles, continuing onward. A few seconds later, Ryder appears, still signaling the danger, excited, and bounding up high on his hind legs.

"What's this about?" Ryder takes off quickly again. "Hey, Boss, I'm moving as fast as I can."

Ryder runs back and forth impatiently. *Whatever it is, it must be just ahead. Thank God.* Stan rests his elbows on his thighs and takes a few seconds to slow his labored breathing. He'd thought he was in better shape.

Up ahead in the thicket, he makes out a large dark shape. He prays he's wrong...it looks like a body.

Ryder is growling and pulling on the pants leg in an effort to wake the unconscious woman.

Panting heavily, Stan hunches over the body. It's a young woman. He brushes the thick strands of dark hair from her face, and guesses that she's in her twenties. Using his skills from past first aid classes, he feels for the carotid pulse in her neck and is relieved that he finds one. It's weak and rapid but she's alive. Her skin is red, and hot.

He shakes her gently and calls to her but there is no response. He rolls her onto her back, checking her arms and legs for any visible injuries, but finds only scratches and bruising. He lifts her shirt looking for any wounds. There is a large dark reddened area in the middle of her left side. *What is her story?*

Her lips are cracked and dry, indicating that she may be dehydrated. *How long has she been here? What do I do now?*

Getting his cell phone out of his pocket, he dials 911 but with his anxiety peaked, he's forgotten there isn't a signal. There will not be any help arriving. This woman's life is in his hands; the actions he takes could mean the difference between whether she lives or dies.

Thinking fast, he makes a plan. He'll mark the area for easy spotting and get the Jeep so he can move her. Then, he'll wrap her side with the Ace bandage in his first aid kit. Once a Boy Scout, always a Boy Scout. After finding shade, he'll try to arouse her enough to get some fluids into her. Addressing her hydration level will determine what he does next. With the ranch more than a day's drive away, waiting to get fluids in her could be dangerous.

He taps his head with his fist in frustration—how far back did he first lose the satellite signal? Three hours? Four? He should have paid attention. If she remains unresponsive, he'll drive until he gets a signal and then give the coordinates for a Medivac helicopter pick-up. It's a good plan.

Stan ties his red handkerchief to the top of the highest sagebrush. He summons Ryder, giving him a good dog, atta-boy affirmation.

"Let's get the Jeep."

Ryder looks at the girl and starts barking again as if uncertain as to where his loyalties lie.

"Okay, I'll get the Jeep. You stay here."

Returning, he drives slower than his racing heart as he fears that in his heightened state, he could run over her. He slams on the brakes when he spots the red bandana on his right. Moving cautiously, he places his right arm under her neck, and pulls her up into a sitting position before sliding his left arm under her thighs. He grunts as he lifts her. His limp worsens with the extra weight, but he awkwardly eases her into the Jeep. Careful to avoid her bruised side, he leans her toward the center and closes the door quickly, then cushions her head with his sleeping bag. He'll drive to a spot with some shade getting her out of the sun. The brief but bumpy ride stirs her and Stan nearly jumps out of his seat in response to her dark brown eyes staring but as though seeing right through him.

"Hi, I'm Stan. I'm here to help. You're going to be fine."

CHAPTER 14

At ArtSmart

The one on your right needs to be a bit higher, dear. Then you'll be able to hang another underneath," says Rita.

"Are you sure?" Gabby turns around on the ladder. "Won't the wall look too crowded if we put another painting under there?"

"Gabby, you need to trust me. I've been doing this a long time. I'll look great. Besides, it's my gallery." She winks.

"I'm sorry. I want everything to be perfect. Nicholas is the best contemporary artist of the decade."

"Yes, he is. Your daddy would have nothing but the best. I can't believe Nicholas accepted the invitation."

"You're right about that. I don't know why I'm so nervous about his visit. It's not like he's going to look at my art."

Rita stands with her hands on her hips. "I think you're wrong. He looks at his art all the time, but as an artist he'll be interested in what other artists are doing. It's true that he is what will bring others into the gallery but they'll admire all the art here."

Rita twirls around, her arms lifted making a reference to all four walls. "And that my dear, includes your artwork. So...let's get these hung. Your new works are different than anything you've exhibited before. It's fresh."

Gabby steps off the ladder. "That's another reason I'm nervous." She studies her works. "It's a new style for me. Maybe they'll hate it."

"Stop being ridiculous, Gabby. Really, child, stretching yourself by trying new techniques keeps you growing. It's a good thing. So many get stuck and never reach out to find their true potential." Rita puts her arms around her as the two continue to survey the wall. "I'll get my level just to make sure everything is perfectly straight. I think we're done here."

Gabby climbs the ladder once again after noticing that one of the paintings hangs crooked. The bell on the door rings, alerting them that someone came into the gallery.

"Hey, ladies, need some help?" says Brett.

"Just like you two to show up after the work is done."

King leans over, kissing Rita. "Sorry, sweetheart. My errands took longer than expected. But the good news is that they're all finished so I am all yours for the rest of the day."

Brett stands next to the ladder and gives Gabby a playful smack on her butt.

"Brett," she scolds.

"Couldn't resist." He smiles, making his dimple more prominent.

King and Rita share a look before he asks, "Ready for lunch? You young'uns gonna join? We're going to that Chinese place just down the way."

Gabby looks lovingly at the older couple. "Sure, Brett can help me clean up here. We'll take some photos, then we'll see you there."

"Sounds great. Don't be too long." Rita smiles at King. "Let me get my purse."

The instant the doorbell jingles, Brett steps on the first rung of the ladder. She turns, putting her arms around his neck.

"And what have you and Daddy been up to?"

"Can't say. It's a surprise." His eyes twinkle.

"You can tell me." She twirls a curl of his hair around her finger and whispers in his ear.

"You, lady, are pretty sexy in those skin-tight jeans but I'm still not tellin'. How about satisfying a hungry man before lunch?"

"Here...now?" She looks around the gallery.

He steps down from the ladder and takes her in his arms. She curls her legs around his body.

"Yep, right now."

She giggles as he carries her into the back room.

CHAPTER 15

Eastern Border of the Ranch

Finding shade in the shadow of a large boulder, Stan carefully lowers the girl onto the padded ground cover he uses under his sleeping bag. Lifting her in and out of the Jeep has caused stress on his knee and he rubs it to dull the pain. He checks her breathing, worried that moving her may have worsened whatever caused that large bruise. He's not sure of the extent of her injuries. He strokes her face, and even with the dirt and grime beneath his fingertips her face is smooth but remains hot.

"Please open your eyes."

She doesn't stir, which heightens his anxiety. Maybe he should be driving and looking for cell phone coverage. What if she dies? Does she have an internal injury? Does she have broken ribs? Is it just a bruise? Her pulse remains weak and rapid. He scans the horizon. He'll never get back to the ranch, and driving in the dark is dangerous, but would that be more dangerous than waiting for morning light? The pros and cons cancel each other. *Think, Stan, think. What should you do?*

Fluids, fluids, she needs fluids—but how? He's not a medic and he has no equipment. Grabbing his titanium straw from his mess kit, he gets some water. Getting behind her and propping her torso on his chest, he places his finger on the end of the straw, delivering a few drops of the liquid under her tongue. It seems to disappear immediately confirming that she is severely dehydrated. He does this small act repeatedly, aware that too much, too fast will cause her to choke.

Taking breaks from that task, he removes her outer clothing and bathes her with cool water to lower her body temperature. Seeing her in her bra and panties reminds him that he hasn't been intimate with a woman in more than a year. He feels guilty for having these thoughts when this young woman's life is in jeopardy. He's pathetic but maybe he's normal too.

He checks his watch and he has been performing these tasks for more than an hour. Time to reevaluate the situation. Her pulse seems stronger and has slowed a bit. He surmises that his efforts are helping. If only she would open her eyes as she did once before. He checks his phone, still no signal. Ryder has been napping in the shade near them.

He goes back to his tasks, alternating drops of water with the straw and wiping her off with cool towels. Then he drops too much water at one time out of the straw and she starts to cough. He turns her face to the side. *Coughing, this is a good sign ... or am I killing her?* The coughing persists and she groans as if in pain, then moans before opening her eyes.

Startled, he reads fear and panic in her expression.

"Hey, it's okay." He tries to calm the terror lurking behind her brown orbs. "You're safe."

She sits erect and peers around as if looking for something familiar. The commotion has stirred Ryder from his sleep and he's next to her side.

Aware that she is in her underwear, she pulls her knees up to her chin. "Where are my clothes?" Stan moves away to give her space in hopes that the distance will calm her anxiety.

"You were overheated and they were covered in dirt. Here, drink this." He hands her the mug of water. "I'll get you a clean shirt, okay?"

With a trembling hand she takes the mug. Her eyes never leave his face. "Who are you?"

"Sorry, I'm Stan Adams. I found you, or rather Ryder found you." He nods toward Ryder and at the sound of his name, Ryder comes over and sniffs the woman. She pets the dog and he cozies up to her.

"He's a good judge of character...seems he likes you." He rubs his chin. "And your name is...?"

She pulls her knees tighter to her chest, there are goosebumps on her skin. "Marie, my name's Marie." Her voice is small and her lips quiver. "Where am I?"

He hands her a flannel shirt from his duffel bag and she eagerly dons it. "You're on the outer border of the King ranch. The main house is about an eight-hour drive from here, more or less." He's been so busy nursing her that the hours have gone by and he's been unaware that the temps have been dropping as the desert is preparing for evening. Heavy, dark clouds have also drifted in from the west. He hands Marie a blanket.

"Thanks. What day is it?"

"Saturday. How long were you out there?"

"I don't know, maybe two days." Her eyes roll upward as if she's thumbing through a file in her head searching for answers.

He fills the mug with more water. "Here, drink some more. How are you feeling?"

"Weak, cold, headache..."

"I was really concerned that you were going to die. So, weak, cold, headache... that's good. We can fix those things." He hands her a protein bar, thinking that the headache and the weakness could be due to a low blood sugar, and gets some Tylenol out of his duffel. "I always carry some... for my leg." He feels the blood rushing to his face. He hopes she thinks it from the sun. Sharing his problems is never easy and they're minor compared to her ordeal.

"We need to use the daylight that's left to get dinner and make camp. Looks like it may rain. You rest and keep drinking. We'll talk later, if you want to."

She nods. "Stan?" He turns to face her. "Might you have something more than water?"

His look causes her concern.

"You know, maybe some juice or soda or something in that Jeep that seems to have a bit of everything."

"Oh yeah, right. There's some juice and beer in the cooler."

"Juice would be great." She lowers her eyes.

"Right, one juice coming up." As he hands her the can of cranberry juice , she studies his face. "Thanks, Stan...for everything."

He nods and turns away quickly. He's anxious to hear her story and prays that she will confide in him. Something seems terribly amiss; however, he must be patient.

Ryder barks and circles around him as if to say, *Hey, what about me?* When the dog's bowl is filled with water, a thirsty Ryder laps it up in short order.

"Sorry, Boss." He strokes his side and the dog licks Stan's hand. "You did good today. really good." And he throws him a treat.

CHAPTER 16

Next, Stan builds a fire to make dinner. Unsure about the state of Marie's stomach that has been days without food, he'll heat chicken broth with rice. Then he drives nails into the foil-wrapped potatoes and positions them on the perimeter of the fire. While these are cooking and before grilling the steak kabobs, he pitches the tent and adds gasoline to the Jeep's tank so it will be ready to go in the morning.

At a distance, the hum of a motor triggers Ryder to stand at attention and Marie's shoulders to straighten as a low-flying Cessna aircraft approaching from the north banks into a sharp left turn. Reaching for his binoculars, Stan observes that the landing wheels are down.

"Well, I'll be," he mutters under his breath.

The plane continues its descent for the nearby landing strip. Engrossed with the plane, Stan ignores Ryder's barking but now spots Marie's back as she races away.

"Hey, wait—where are you going?"

Stan runs and catching up, he tugs her arm. "Marie, wait, what's wrong?"

"They're here. We need to go. Now. Please, Stan, they'll kill me. Let me go. Please." She sobs hysterically. "I knew they would find me."

"Marie, who are you talking about?"

Her eyes are as big as saucers. "Them."

"Who is *them*? Help me here, Marie. Who are they?"

"The men, the human traffickers, the drug lord." Her eyes dart back and forth and her body shakes uncontrollably.

Stan pulls her in tight. "Marie, I'm here. I won't let them get you."

"You can't save me. They'll kill you too." She turns to run again.

"Marie, stop. If that's true, we'll get farther in the Jeep than we will on foot."

She halts, processing what he said. "Why would you help me? You'll put yourself in danger. They'll kill you." She clasps her hands together. "I can't let you do this. You don't know me."

"You're right. I don't know you. But Ryder likes you and he's a great judge of character."

This statement causes a nervous chuckle and she places her hands on her bruised side. "You're my Indiana Jones. Is that it, you're going to save me?"

"What?" Stan scratches his head.

"Never mind. You're right. The Jeep is faster."

"Come with me."

Reluctantly, but obediently she follows him to the top of the ridge and with the binoculars he views the plane that landed. At the

90

end of the runway, close to the plane, two vehicles have arrived. He squints to count the men but he's too far away.

"Here, you watch them. Don't let them out of your sight." He hands her the binoculars. "I'll be back, I need my drone. You got this?"

She bites her lip and shakes her head.

He hopes that by giving her an assignment, she'll stay put. With haste, he returns with the drone and sighs in relief that she didn't flee.

"What are they doing?"

"They're standing there."

"Are the two trucks there?"

"Yes."

He removes the drone from the carrying case and launches the quadcopter up, flying it in the direction of the airstrip. Keeping the drone at a safe and low distance, but close enough to hopefully read the serial numbers on the plane and the license plates with the zoom function. He's careful to position the drone and with any luck may capture the faces of the men as well. Maybe with the advancements in facial recognition, the authorities will be able to identify them.

Marie says with urgency, "Stan, the trucks...the trucks are leaving." She's pacing back and forth.

"Okay, let's watch where they go. Can you do that?"

She holds up the binoculars again with shaky hands.

Quick to hit the automatic return-home switch on the drone's controls, he leaves the base with Marie and runs to the Jeep. If her story is accurate, these men are dangerous and great caution should be exercised. If the plane takes off in this direction, the pilot could spot the Jeep. With his only two tarps, he does his best to disguise the vehicle. He's also relieved that the fire is low and with the remaining daylight it should not attract attention.

Marie watches as the vehicles drive in the opposite direction away from their camp and gives a deep sigh. Her letdown is short as she jumps when she hears the plane's engines start, turns around and picks up speed to take off. Stan hears it too so he rushes toward Marie.

"Get down, " he yells. "I don't want them to see us." He pulls her from her standing position on the ridge, down into the sagebrush. He covers her body with his as the plane flies overheard. These actions add fuel to her previous adrenalin rush.

He remembers her bruised side. "I'm sorry. I forgot, did I hurt you?"

"We need to leave." She grabs his shirt and her high-pitched voice is a clue that she is on the verge of hysterics. "We need to leave, now."

"Whoa there, pretty lady. Stop, take a breath." He grips tight to her arm as his body can't take running after her again. "You watched them leave, right? Which direction were they going?" He pauses and then answers for her. "Away from us, right? It'll be dark in just an hour. It would be foolish to drive around in the dark. We're safe; they're gone. They went the other way."

Watching her wide eyes, he offers more reassurance. "They didn't see us. You're safe."

"How can you be so sure?"

"I'm sure. Okay? We'll leave first thing in the morning. It's going to be all right. Really, can you trust me? I need you to trust me."

She sniffles and nods her head.

"The drone got some great footage and we'll get it into the proper hands. I got this."

Her expression is still panic-ridden.

"Hey, there's nothing we can do tonight. Let's get some dinner; get some shut-eye and we'll be on our way bright and early, before the sun greets us. Deal?"

She wipes her tears on his shirt. He places his arms around her frail frame and she leans into his chest. With his chin on the top of her head, he says, "I won't let anything happen to you." And he means every word. It's been a long time since he was strong.

Stan takes his drone from its base and puts it in the case. There'll be plenty of time to look at the footage later. Now, with dark clouds approaching, they need dinner before the rain starts. Perhaps the plane was quick to leave because of this storm. Whatever the reason, he'll try to act nonchalant. However, after placing the drone in the Jeep, he pauses and retrieves his revolver from the glove box, checks the chambers, and places it in his backpack. He needs to be ready, just in case things don't pan out the way he explained to the fragile woman in his care. Be prepared is the Boy Scout motto he lives by.

* * * *

As he guessed, Marie's stomach isn't up for steak but she eagerly eats the chicken broth and rice. After the meal, she asks for a bucket of water. He hands her his toiletries and even gives her permission to use his toothbrush. This makes her smile. It's the first time she lets down her guard.

He catches glimpses of her grooming and he's intrigued watching her bend over at the waist using his comb through her thick brown locks. She is pretty and has a tomboyish demeanor underneath that fragile exterior. Watching her after this panic stage will prove interesting. Exactly who is she? How did she get here? He needs answers.

He sits back on his tripod stool with a beer and tries to recount the events of the day. It was interesting and unexpected and more adventure than anticipated. His day has proved to be unbelievable as well as unthinkable.

Dusk is settling in early as the dark clouds hide the sun setting. Marie returns wearing his flannel shirt and his sweatpants that would easily double around her waist.

"How are you?"

"Much better. Thanks for letting me use your stuff."

"Glad to help a lady in need."

"I owe you a new comb. I bent some of the teeth trying to get the knots out of my hair. Sorry." She turns from him.

"Not a problem. Combs can be replaced. Here, have a seat." He motions toward the second tripod. "Are you ready to tell me exactly what's going on?"

Sitting close to him with the fire highlighting her face, she takes a deep breath. "I was kidnapped... along with my best friend, Alexa."

OMG, he thinks, as he leans forward a bit more.

Marie tells scattered bits of her story, stopping frequently and turning away. Only some of his questions are answered. He doesn't wish to press her.

"I am so sorry," he says. "I had no idea." He shakes his head.

"I need to find Alexa. They took her away." Her voice breaks. "She's so beautiful—thin, the perfect figure, long, blond hair. I always envied her looks and how easily she attracted men." She breaks down crying again.

He doesn't have a Kleenex and hates when women cry. Something deep inside him seems to tear apart. "This farm, do you know where it is?"

She's bent over with her hands covering her face and shakes her head.

"What all did they grow there?"

"Mostly marijuana, some vegetables, chickens, food for us to eat."

He has so many questions: how many guards were there; were they armed; how often did the boss come? She does her best to answer all of them.

"You kept saying that they would kill us. Did you ever see them kill anyone?"

She nods and wipes a tear from her cheek before responding. "One woman tried to escape—the guards shot her, right in front of us. Then there were the two guards that were working that night. The boss, he went up to one of them, lifted his gun to the man's forehead and fired. The man fell over and the blood and brains splattered...I'll never forget."

Stan reaches to provide comfort. "I'm so sorry to have you go through that again, but I need to know what we're up against. You're safe now. We can take care of this. We have something they don't. We have Wayne King."

She looks into his face. "Wayne King? Who is that?

"He's the best. You'll meet him tomorrow." Stan pats her shoulder. "You're going to be fine, just fine."

The night sky delivers rain as the dark clouds promised. The drops come big and hard. He ushers Marie into the tent with Ryder at her heels.

He covers the supplies to keep them dry and wraps himself in a tarp, keeping his backpack close. Cold, wet, and shivering, Stan sits holding the tarp above his head. The rain blows in heavy sheets across the plains. Bad news for a guy with only a tarp for protection, but also good news as no one in his right mind would be out on a night like tonight. It was a wise decision to stay the night even though he did have some second thoughts but kept his concerns to himself. No use upsetting Marie in her fragile state. Along with the rain cooler temperatures have come. Cold and wet, he's miserable. He glances at the tent. Ryder's in there warm and dry, that lucky dog. Stan pulls the tarp closer.

Marie parts the break in the door of the tent and her heart goes out in empathy for this kind stranger. She owes him a debt of gratitude as he saved her life. Without water, she could possibly be dead. She owes him and because of her, he's out there in the wet and cold.

Her movement wakes Ryder and he yelps. "You're right," she murmurs. "We can't leave him out there."

She parts the tent door wider. "Hey, Stan." No response so she yells louder as she isn't going out there. "Hey, Stan!"

He looks in her direction. "Something wrong?"

She motions with her finger. "Come here."

He hesitates but complies. "What do you need?" The rain drips off the tarp as he lowers his head toward her.

"Come in here. There's room." She lifts the tent door open wider.

"I can't." He backs away.

"You're going to catch cold. How can my Indiana Jones save me, if he's sick? Please, I'll feel better. Ryder agrees."

Stan looks around as if to get approval from an absent audience before entering the tent. He leaves his tarp outside to keep everything inside as dry as possible. Sitting, he takes his boots off before setting them near the edge but careful not to have them touch the sides of the tent as then the wetness would come through the material. The backpack rests on top of the boots.

"Well, this is cozy." His voice shakes a bit and he blows breath into his hands to warm them.

"Here, I can move over a few more inches. You're getting me wet—take off that shirt. And you should rid yourself of those wet pants as well."

"But—"

"Stan, it's dark. I'll turn over. I promise, I won't look."

If he could see her face, he would see that her eyes are smiling. "I have my clothes on so it's not like we're naked and touching or anything like that."

It's really against his better judgment but she's right. Carefully he sheds his wet clothes and he still shivers. This is embarrassing.

"Are you getting in?" She unzips the sleeping bag. "Your shyness is noted as honorable, but this situation calls for practicality over what's proper. You asked me to trust you. I'm trusting you, okay? Unusual circumstances call for strange measures. I admit this is weird for me too."

It's awkward but she's right. His wet clothes would only drop his body temperature faster. Careful not to push against her too hard, he scoots into the sleeping bag next to her.

As much as he hates to admit it, this is one hundred percent more comfortable. After a few moments, his shivering stops and he's getting quite cozy, maybe too cozy. Ryder is curled up tightly at the foot of the sleeping bag.

"Are we good?" Her whisper breaks the sound of the rain on the tent.

"Yeah, I'm good. Are you good?"

She reaches for his hand and brings it forward around her waist and gently kisses it. "My hero. Now, I'm good. 'Nite."

Minutes later her breathing is regular and even. *Thank God she's asleep. Am I dreaming? What a crazy, crazy day.* He can calm down some and give up the macho I-got-this attitude. Truth be told, he's scared; however, he is more afraid of lying next to Marie than he is of the men who may come after them. The experience she's been through should have created trust issues; instead she's extending total trust in him. It's confusing. He speculates that maybe her dehydrated state is responsible for this erratic behavior or perhaps this kidnapping story is a lie and perhaps she escaped from a mental hospital.

With all of these unsettling thoughts swimming through his mind, he's uncertain if he'll get any rest. But he's wrong—the melodic tune of the rain on the tent, the warmth of their bodies mingled together, and a short time later the matched rhythm of their breathing makes them as if they are one in this surreal adventure.

CHAPTER 17

The next morning, Ryder is the first to stir. He licks Stan's face and pulls on the sleeping bag as if to say *wake up*, one of their familiar games. He finds Marie's face and gives her a lick also.

"Oh, nasty puppy breath." She pushes him away.

"Sorry, it's his way of saying good morning."

She rubs her eyes and then stretches with her arms above her head, accidently hitting Stan. "Sorry." She pulls her arm back.

As feared, he's woken with his standard morning arousal. He prays she's unaware.

"Close your eyes."

"Why?"

"'Cause I'm getting up," he says.

"Do I have to?"

"Yes, you have to."

She giggles.

He unzips the bag and then opens wide the tent door. The cooler air rushes in but at least the rain has stopped. He grabs his wet clothes, boots, and backpack on his way out.

Marie cannot control her curiosity and watches him as he crawls from the tent. Her smile is wide.

Stan and Ryder survey the landscape. The night's heavy rain has turned the desert floor into mud. Walking to the Jeep, he gets his waterproof bag and dons dry jeans, shirt and fresh socks. The firewood didn't survive as well, as it accidentally got wet since he used the tarp to disguise the Jeep. It seems the morning has its own plan. Retrieving his small gas stove, he sets a pot of water on it to boil.

"Coffee in ten minutes. Only oatmeal this morning. Hope that's okay," he says, facing the tent.

She emerges still dressed in his flannel shirt and sweatpants. "I like oatmeal." She turns and walks away.

"Hey, where are you going?"

"A lady needs her privacy." She laughs.

"Sorry, I wasn't thinking. I won't look."

"If you do, you're a pervert."

He shakes his head. In their brief time together, statements that come out of her mouth surprise him. He should have offered her some toilet paper. Too late now as she will surely think him a pervert if he tries to follow with it.

When she returns, they share their simple breakfast and while she cleans up, he breaks camp. The sun had broken the horizon at least a half hour ago. They should be on their way. He checks the airfield with his binoculars and strains to see the four-by-four vehicles. His vision field is empty. No sign of the men.

"You ready?" He stands peering. "Ryder, where'd you go?"

"I saw him over there by a rabbit hole or something like that."

He calls his name again and whistles. Ryder comes bounding out of the brush with briars on his ears again.

****

An hour later, driving through the prairie in the direction of the ranch house, Stan notices that Marie is quiet and staring as if deep in thought.

"What are you thinking?"

"Nothing," she sighs.

"I find that hard to believe. Tell me about yourself. You have any family?

"It's a boring story."

"We have all day, Marie. You can take as much time as you'd like. I'll tell you if it's a boring story." He winks.

She adjusts her position in the seat before speaking. "My grand-parents left Mexico and came to live in California, near San Diego. My grandmother cleaned houses and my grandfather was a garden-er. My mother spoke English well enough to get into school. She met my dad in high school. I'm the second generation to be born a United States citizen and I'm the second in my family to graduate from college."

"And you graduated from Southern Cal with a psychology de-gree." He remembers from their conversation last night.

"A master's degree," she's quick to correct.

"Impressive. So now what's your plan?"

She leans back in the seat. "I hope to get a job back in San Diego near my family. I have an older brother but he lives in the San Francisco Bay area. He lives with his girlfriend. My parents disapprove but they can't stop him. He's into computer stuff."

"What kind of a job does a psychologist do?"

"This last semester I interned at a veterans hospital. I was promised a job but then they lost government funding for some of the programs and the offer went away. Alexa and I are both unemployed so we thought we would vacation a few weeks in Cancun. Celebrate our graduation and brainstorm as to where to find that perfect job in that perfect place. It seems like a silly dream now after all that has happened.

"I need to find Alexa. Can your Wayne King help with that?" Her eyes and voice plead urgency.

He reaches over and squeezes her hand. "I promise we'll do everything we can. But first we need to get there."

His kind gesture makes her bite her lower lip and a tear rolls down her cheek.

"Thanks." She squeezes his hand in return. She wants to confide in him, tell her whole story, but whenever she tries the words get stuck in her throat.

Reliving the events in her mind, she recalls the shackles and how she tried relentlessly to tear the rope with her teeth. As her memory takes her deeper, her heart starts pounding in her ears, getting louder with each second and then panic rises and she can't breathe. She's not ready, so instead of sharing, she stares at the passing landscape. For the rest of the hour, they drive in silence.

When they come to a level clearing, he brakes. "We still have four hours to go, so how about some lunch. Nothing fancy, just whatever is left. Hope you like peanut butter and crackers 'cause that's all

I got." He digs deeper into his backpack and lifts out a gooey half-eaten protein bar. "Except for this." He throws it to Ryder.

"Whatever, it will be great." She scans the nearby landscape. "I need to find the little girls' room."

"Ryder will go with you. Here's some TP and watch out for rattlesnakes. They're out this time of year."

She calls over her shoulder, "Gee thanks for that," and continues on her mission. Before fixing lunch, his cell has three bars so he makes a call to King, briefly explaining their situation, and uses the last of his spare gas to fill the tank.

After their quick lunch, Stan offers Marie some sunscreen and one of his old baseball caps. "I prefer the sun over the rain but we'll get burnt quickly. Here, these should help."

As she's busy applying the greasy white protectant, he shudders as though a cool breeze whipped right through him. Unable to see them, he can feel the presence of goosebumps on his arms and legs. He mentally goes through the list of what ifs...what if Marie had remained unconscious and he had to make this trip in the dark and with the rain, what if she required more medical attention that he was unable to provide? What if she had died? Stopping this negative thought pattern, he thinks of his three gratitudes for today:

He's thankful for the sun and clear skies. Driving in the likes of the storm last night would not have been pleasant.

He's grateful that Ryder found Marie.

He's grateful for a recovering Marie.

Everything evaluated, the entire situation has turned out much better than he initially feared. He prays, thanking God for placing him in the right place at the right time. He smiles bringing to mind the terms that she used for him—"my Indiana Jones, my hero." It has a nice ring to it.

Finished applying the sunscreen, they load up the Jeep and start the last leg of this journey. During this part of the ride she focuses on Stan. She reads his seriousness from the creases in his brow. The ride is bumpy and Stan's concentrating to avoid the waterholes and ruts.

"You look deep in thought. Care to share?"

Her teeth are white and straight. He never noticed that before; maybe it's the sunlight.

"Just thankful that things have worked out so well."

She smiles. "Your turn. Tell me about you."

"There's not much to tell."

"That answer didn't work for me so it's not going to work for you. You walk with a cane, why?"

He hangs his head before answering. *Why does every conversation involve my leg?*

"I had a motorcycle accident last fall."

"I ride. You still ride?"

"I haven't yet. Not since the accident but I think about it."

"Oh, you have boots, are you a cowboy?"

"Not exactly. This is kind of temporary. I was a motorcycle mechanic in DC, and before that I was a lawyer."

"That's a surprise. You don't act like a lawyer. Well, none that I've ever met."

He looks at her, concerned. "Why is that?"

"You have this rugged edge about you. Maybe it's because we're out here but I can't imagine you in a suit sitting behind a desk."

"I have to admit sitting behind a desk wasn't for me but the education paid off. I use some of that knowledge at the Equine Assisted Therapy Program. Writing contracts and setting up accounts. My stepsister founded the business a few months ago. I'm helping her get it started."

"I studied about that therapy in school. I would like to see the center and observe some patients. Can you show me?"

"Sure, would love to. The therapy has done wonders to help with my rehab. I enjoy riding and love the horses. It's better than hitting the gym every day because you're outside, breathing fresh air."

"Is there a Mrs. Stan?"

"No." His gaze leaves her face and the blood travels to his ears. He prays she doesn't notice. "I haven't had much luck when it comes to women."

"A handsome, smart guy like you, I can't imagine." She props her hand on her chin.

"How about you? You got a boyfriend somewhere worried about you?"

She giggles. "We broke up a few months ago. I'm sure he wasn't my Mr. Right but we had fun."

Stan would like to ask more but the old windmill is in view. "We're getting there. See that windmill? That landmark means we're just a few hours out. When we stopped for our gourmet lunch of peanut butter crackers, I had cell phone coverage and called the ranch. They'll be looking for us."

From this point forward, he acts as Marie's personal tour guide, reminding him of his past when Gabby showed him the ranch. That was almost a year ago and he pinches his lips as he reminisces about everything he's been through since then. That day with Gabby seems a much longer time ago.

They get to a pasture of grazing cattle, and he points out a few facts about cattle, before they travel the road along the river. He noticed that Marie started holding her bruised side shortly after lunch, but there wasn't much he could do to smooth the ride. However, now at least they're on a dirt path and that will be somewhat smoother.

He stops at a break in the trees where the river is in full view and turns off the ignition. "Hey, you okay? Let me get you some Tylenol. You should have taken some before we started out."

"I don't want to complain. You've been so great." She hangs her head.

He gets the pills from his backpack and gives her his water bottle.

"Thanks. That should help."

"I need to tell you about the family. Okay? It can be a bit confusing but they're all really great people. You'll like them." He stands and comes to her side of the Jeep, opening the door.

"Come, let's stretch our legs." She follows closely as they meander on the riverbank.

"All of this land that we have been driving on is owned by Mr. Wayne King. He's now my stepfather. My mother, Rita, and he were married last April. He has a daughter, Gabriella, whose husband is Brett." Stan turns away and clears his throat before starting again. "Then there's Jamie and Rusty. They're the caretakers of the ranch but they live in the main house and are considered family. Rusty is the ranch foreman and Jamie is the housekeeper and cook, and, well, she's the glue that keeps this whole family and ranch running. Anyway, they're going to be all over you and shower you with so much attention. You can't say, I didn't warn you."

"They sound like wonderful people."

"For the most part, they are but every family has its problems."

"That's why I'll have a job. If there were no problems, there's no need for a psychologist." She giggles. "But look at me—I'm a mess."

"After all you've been through, that's the least of your worries. You look fine."

"You would say that."

"However, I am sensitive to a lady's needs."

Retrieving his phone from his pocket, he sends a text.

"What is that all about?'

"I asked Jamie to round up a set of clothes from Gabby. You're a little smaller than Gab but her clothes will fit you better than my sweats." He laughs. "Anything else, fair lady?"

He bows as if she were a queen. "I warned you. They're going to love you. Ready to meet them? Let's go. " He reaches for her hand and leads her back to the Jeep.

Mindful of her sore side, he pushes gently on the gas and knowing that his time alone with her will be over in less than an hour makes him a bit sad.

CHAPTER 18

The King Ranch

As they pull up the drive to the ranch house, Jamie's concern is apparent as she bounds down the steps with Gabby close at her heels.

"It's about time. We've been worried sick. Where's this poor girl?"

He pulls the keys from the ignition and opens the door. "She's fine."

Jamie points to her apron pocket. "Got my pistol right here. Cleaned it up as soon as I heard. I'll be ready for 'em." She nods.

Stan puts his arm around Jamie. "I appreciate your spunk but keep that thing in your pocket. You'll frighten Marie."

He looks at Marie, his eyes dancing. "She like my second mother—tough, but has a heart of gold. Marie, this is Jamie. Jamie, meet Marie."

Jamie rounds the back bumper and gets to Marie's door. "You poor thing."

Marie stands holding onto her side. "I'm fine."

"You're moving a bit slow there. Don't worry, the doctor is on his way to check you out. Can't be takin' any chances."

Marie says, "I'm okay. Really, there's no need. Thank goodness for Ryder and Stan."

"Just to be on the safe side. Besides, he likes my cookin'. Come along, child." Jamie ushers Marie to the porch steps. "I've got sandwiches, fresh lemonade and cookies."

Stan lifts his brow. "Cookies, I love cookies."

"Well, come along. Where are my manners? Marie, this is Gabby."

Gabby reaches out her hand to Marie to welcome her. "So glad to meet you. What an ordeal. The sheriff will be here and we can all hear about it then. I'm glad that the boys found you."

Stan runs his fingers through his hair; he's bothered about being referred to as a boy. He steps next to Marie and places his hand on the small of her back in an act of protection.

Then Jamie says, "After our snack, Gabby's going to take you to her house. You're going to love it. She and Brett just moved in. It's brand new and so pretty the way Gabby's decorated it. You'll be more comfortable there than here." Jaime stops to open the porch door. "Besides, she has a full closet full of clothes and I'm sure she can fix you right up."

Stan can't believe his ears. He's responsible for Marie; he needs to keep her close. He can't fulfill that obligation if she is with Gabby and Brett. And it's hard to imagine what Gabby will reveal if the two women get caught up in girl talk. He'll pull Jamie to the side later and have a conversation. This is not a good plan.

As Jamie steps over the threshold Marie asks, "Can I use your phone? I need to call my parents and let them know I'm okay. They didn't expect to hear from me in Mexico. I won't go into any detail; however, I do want to touch base with them."

"Of course, dear." Jamie shoves Marie along and Stan is left standing on the porch. He's lost control.

He turns back to the Jeep. He gets his duffel with the dirty clothing and his cane, but he'll unload the rest of his supplies later. He calls for Ryder, who leaped out of the vehicle and ran toward the barn as soon as it stopped. Filling Ryder's dish on the porch with fresh water, he calls again. Ryder comes bounding around from the path that leads to the barn.

"Hey, Boss, we men need to stick together. I fear the women are taking over."

CHAPTER 19

Stan checks his appearance in the full-length mirror. Reaching for his comb from the bathroom counter, he gives his hair one last touch. He wants to look his best.

It has been a whirlwind around the ranch house these past two hours since he and Marie arrived. First, she contacted her parents giving them an abridged version. She acted very matter-of-factly but her parents could read between the spoken words and imagined that the worst of ordeals happened to their daughter. The Facetime call seemed to calm them enough to curb their original reaction of hopping on a plane headed for Texas, as they could see she was in good hands with the Kings.

Next, in spite of Stan's protests, Marie left with Gabby. He'll just have to accept that but his surrender does not mean he's on board with the plan. Having Gabby and Marie together he's certain will bring him future troubles. Plus, he doesn't trust Brett. Will he make negative comments about Stan? He'll have to believe that his loving stepsister and her husband will keep their opinions to themselves.

The smells from the kitchen are wafting up the stairs. It seems Jamie is going out of her way to impress their dinner guests.

Wearing his best plaid shirt and his newest black jeans, he realizes Jamie isn't the only one eager to please. His nervousness baffles him a bit as Marie has just been through hell and he's here thinking of ways to impress her. She didn't seem to mind that he held her hand earlier. Holding dear to his memory from last night, he's perplexed by her boldness urging him to slide into the sleeping bag next to her. Is he reading more into that gesture than its due?

With the sound of an engine outside his window, he pulls the curtains back to find Brett's convertible pulling up in front. He stands to the side and back a bit so as not to be seen. Immediately pulling in behind them are the sheriff's truck and the doctor's car. He already sent the footage from the drone to the sheriff's department but they still asked to question him. Marie will also endure long hours of examination. From his experience as an attorney, he knows that they will do individual interviews and then the authorities will compare notes. He's up for it; whatever it takes to bring these monsters to justice. Since they all arrived together and from the ranch road, it occurs to him that they came from Gabby's place. If they already took Marie's statement, he would have liked to be present.

The chatter outside is getting louder and Stan sees King shaking hands with Marie. Stan needs to get down there fast. He tucks his shirt into his pants and rechecks his profile in the mirror, making an effort to flatten his stomach. The gesture is a reminder that he hasn't been working out routinely. Taking his cane that rests behind the chair, he anticipates a walk with Marie after dinner. He wants her to himself, and part of him wishes that they had stayed out on the prairie.

Stan makes a conscientious effort to navigate the curved stairs without favoring his leg and without his cane. He stops midway to observe the party gathered below. His eyes scan the room but he can't find Marie. He was sure they just came in the front door. The sheriff is speaking to King.

Stan confronts his mother. "Where's Marie?" There is a sense of urgency in his tone.

"Honey, not to worry. Your gal is with Doctor Henry. He's examining her, that's all."

Rita rubs his arm. "You seem very protective of her. Reminds me of when you were a child. You found that little gray kitten and you didn't want to allow anyone to pet it."

"I remember. It was the neighbor's. The kitten had escaped from the box where his brothers and sisters lived. I had to give it back." He smiles at the memory.

"If I remember right, we had to almost tear it out of your arms. You wanted to keep it but it was too small, it needed its mother." She looks to him very lovingly. "I'm very proud to be your mother. You saved her. "

"I happen to be in the right place at the right time. Anyone would have done what I did."

"But it wasn't anyone, it was you." She pulls on his arm again and gazes into his eyes. "Want a beer? I put some mugs in the freezer."

He nods and she leaves his side.

The sheriff takes this opportunity to approach. "Thanks for the drone footage; our staff's reviewing. We should have some answers tomorrow. I have a few more questions for Marie."

"You already spoke with her?

"Yes, we went to the Matthews house first. It's best to get her story as soon as possible. I'll conduct your interview in the morning. Is that good for you?

"Whatever you need," Stan says. "How was she...did she remember everything? I should have been there."

The sheriff puts his arm on Stan's shoulder. "Hey, you give your point of view tomorrow. I wanted it straight for the victim before others had a chance to influence her. You know how these things go." He pats him on the back again.

Rita arrives with two mugs of beer, one for the sheriff and one for Stan.

The sheriff looks at his watch, lifting the mug. "I'm officially off duty. Thanks for the dinner invite. I haven't had the pleasure of enjoying one of Jamie's homecooked meals in a while."

"I'll keep that in mind and extend more social invitations without the need of a crisis," Rita says. "Thanks for your promptness."

"Sure thing, ma'am." He tips his hat.

Meanwhile, Doc Henry and Marie exit King's office and mingle with the others. Marie looks as if she's the belle of the ball, instead of a woman who barely escaped death twenty-four hours ago. The transformation is astonishing. Her brunette locks fall softly to her mid-back, except for one side, held back by a silver barrette exposing the curve of her face. Her shiny hair glistens even in the diminished light of the early evening. Her skin still glows pink from sun exposure. With make-up, her eyes look twice the size that he remembers and her lips are full and shiny with gloss. On her ears are large hoops. She's dressed in a full skirt that flows to cover her feet. Lastly, she wears a creamy lace blouse, cut to show a hint of the rise of her breasts. Stan thinks her stunning.

His stares catch her attention and she glances in his direction, giving a small wave. He starts to narrow the distance between them.

She's first to speak. "You clean up nicely."

"You, the same. Are you doing okay?" He leans to hug her. "You smell good too."
She reaches for his hand.

"I'm getting there. It's exhausting talking about it. I can't thank you enough for all that you have done."

"Anyone would have done the same." He feels the heat rushing to the top of his head. At the same time his nose detects the familiar scent of Chanel. Gabby stands next to him as if they are a team.

"Seems you're quite the hero." Gabby takes a sip of her wine. "Marie told us her story. It really is incredible. You and Ryder being there at just the right time, in the right place. It's truly amazing. This is the stuff that makes a novel." It seems to Stan as if she's skeptical as her voice lacks sincerity.

"It was very fortunate and we are both so thankful."

During this exchange he steps closer to Marie, leaving Gabby as the one standing alone. Marie must have gotten the same vibes. She places her arm through his and with a twinkle in her eye she explains, "I call him my Indiana Jones, my hero. He was the answer to my prayers."

"Is that so?" Gabby lifts her glass. "Here's to our hero."

"I hope your dad can help find my friend, Alexa."

"When my daddy puts his mind to something, he doesn't stop."

A clicking of a spoon on a glass quiets the room and King speaks.

"Welcome to the King Ranch. I want to thank Sheriff Mac and Doc Henry for their quick response. I want to give a special welcome to Marie. We're so glad you're safe and I understand Doc Henry has given you an almost perfect health score—a few bruises and scratches but you'll be like new in a few days.

"I take great pride in my land and I will put a stop to this shocking news," he says firmly. "I'll get to the bottom of this with the help of the sheriff and his department. I will not have my land used for criminal activity. These men will get what they deserve, mark my words. Lastly, a big thanks to Stan for his assertiveness and survival skills. Great work out there. You make us proud."

These words of praise coming from the honorable Wayne King taste as sweet as honey on Texas cornbread. It's the first time since his stint in rehab that Stan feels respect and value.

CHAPTER 20

Dinner has a full table, which always makes King happy. He's one for gatherings and celebrations. He loves to listen to stories and better yet, tell them: the longer the dinner, the more vivid the stories, the louder King laughs. Stan has witnessed this many a time over the past year.

Seeing Gabby quiet during these gatherings piques Stan's curiosity. He wonders if Gabby, who shows no signs of this extrovert trait, takes after her mother. The only time he recalls Gabby actively participating in a dinner discussion was the night he told the story of them together in DC. That was at the peak of his reliance on drugs and alcohol, which caused a lapse in good judgement. He's sorry for these actions that created an upset between Gabby and Brett, though he never apologized. Now, he observes the newlyweds as they sit and frequently reach for each other's hand. He surmises that they're happy.

Marie's giggle gets his attention, bringing him back to the present. She's conversing with the doctor and he wonders about the subject of their conversation. Stan's annoyed with the seating arrangement. After King's toast, the doctor got in front of Stan when Jamie rang the dinner bell, taking the seat on Marie's right. Stan had to settle for the only remaining seat at the table, two seats away from Marie. Since they arrived at the ranch, one thing after another has prevented them from having any time together. He'll need to fix that.

Later at dusk walking to the barn to show Marie the horses, they stroll side by side. In the crisp evening breeze, she shivers, then wraps the blanket around her tightly. "Here, I can help with that." He places his arm around her shoulders to help hold the blanket in place. "What do you think of our little homestead?"

"It's quite amazing. Little... not the word I would use."

"It can be a bit overwhelming. I remember my first visit. It was last spring for my mother's wedding."

She turns to face him. "Your mother got married here. That's romantic."

"It was nice. Small, just a few hundred neighbors and friends." He laughs. "I don't believe that King has ever done anything less than grand. What did you think of him?"

"He seems so authentic, exactly how one would picture a Texas rancher. He's handsome, distinguished with that full head of white hair and white beard. Sort of reminds me of Kenny Rogers."

"And Rita?"

"That's not fair, you're asking me about your mother?" She puts her hands on her hips. "Okay, for you, I'll answer. She's happy with her life and doesn't care for small talk. She goes right to the point. By the way, you don't look like her."

"People tell me I favor my father. He was in the Army. He died years ago."

"I'm sorry."

"After that and for a long time, it was my mother, me, and my younger brother, Will. He lives in DC. He met Ella, Gabby's best friend, at my mother's wedding. They're expecting a baby in a few months. Everyone is connected in some way, almost like a knot." He twists his wrists and hands as if fashioning a knot. "Everyone is finding love and happiness. Don't get me wrong, I'm happy that my mother finally moved forward with her life and that Will and Ella found each other."

"Sounds as though you're feeling left behind.

"There you go, analyzing me."

"Sorry, a career hazard. Did Gabby and Brett also get married here?"

"No, they got married in town at the big new art gallery."

"They seem happy." She stops walking and studies his face. "What's up between you and Gabby?"

"I'm not sure I know what you're talking about."

"She's warm and friendly; however, she's cooler to you and you act differently around her. Your interaction is interesting."

"After one dinner, you're analyzing her and me? Wow, this is becoming annoying."

She smiles and starts walking ahead of him. "I've been with you long enough to know when something's off. That's all." She turns to face him again. "Don't be mad. For the record, just because I asked doesn't mean you have to tell. It's just an observation. And now, I know from both your expression and your response that my observation was correct." She runs on ahead.

"That's not fair." He shakes his head. *Is it that obvious?* "Hey, wait for me."

After introducing all of the horses to Marie, they exit the barn and walk toward the corral. The big Texas night sky grabs their attention.

She stands peering for a few moments. "It's beautiful. So many stars."

"I had my telescope along on the trip, but I didn't get to use it."

"And I'm sorry for earlier and I'm sorry about the stargazing." She rubs his arm.

"I'm not. Finding you was more important. Besides, the weather was pretty bad. I'm not complaining about that either. I can't believe you invited me into your sleeping bag."

"What else was I to do? Leave you out there shivering and wet?"

"Like I said, I'm not complaining. Hey, are we going to share this part of the story or is this between us?"

"You're concerned about other people's reactions. You're concerned they will judge me or you. You're being protective of my reputation. That's sweet, but not an issue. People will think what they want to think. They weren't there. Stan, stop worrying." They walk in silence.

"It's special now thinking back, but at the time it was weird." She giggles.

"If you felt weird, think of stepping into my shoes. Or should I say, getting out of them." He stops walking and turns to her. "You're right, others may judge but they weren't there. Seriously, it was the most selfless, caring act and reveals your true character. You, Marie, are a good person."

"Guess I'm not the only one making observations."

"And I don't have a psychology degree."

They meander along the path and she continues gazing upward.

"I still have that telescope and since I didn't use it, I have an idea. Tomorrow's forecast is supposed to be similar. We'll drive to the hill over there," he points toward the east, "and I'll set up the telescope and we can check out the planets and galaxies, and maybe even catch some falling stars. Would you like that?"

"Sounds more like a date." She smiles.

He remains quiet.

"Yes, I would like that. It's a date."

He sighs in relief.

From the ranch house, Brett calls, "We're taking off in ten minutes."

"Coming right up," Stan yells.

Then he looks to Marie. "You've had a long day. You must be tired."

"Truth is, I am tired. These past few days have been a whirlwind. This whole ordeal..."

"Do you need anything?"

"Me, no. Gabby's house is great. I love the setting with the oak trees with the lake. It's a paradise."

"Do you have my number? Of course, you don't. You don't have a cell phone."

"Stan, I'll be fine. Gabby does have a home phone and there is one in my room. You can call me to say good night in an hour or so. That's if you still want to talk to me, even though you think I'm annoying."

"You got me there. I would like to call you."

"Me too. We should get going. I don't want to keep my ride waiting."

"You're right."

They walk from the darkness into the light mounted on the flagpole, where the Kings stand and observe the sheriff's and doctor's vehicle lights disappearing down the lane out the gates to the main road.

CHAPTER 21

S tan's sleep was off and on all night. At five a.m. he hops out of bed when he hears others stirring. King is always one that's up before the sun. He's sure his mother is still sleeping. As he enters the kitchen, King is making coffee as Jamie's usually not at her post for another half-hour. Stan opens the back door for Ryder.

"Sheriff Mac will be here around eight. I think he wants Jamie's breakfast. Can't say I blame him. I'm glad you're up, gives us a chance to talk. What is your take on all of this?"

"I'm not sure I understand what you are asking." Stan scratches his head.

"I didn't want to mention anything in front of the others, but what were you thinking, going all that way by yourself? Maybe you should have let someone know where you were going. You could have gotten yourself killed."

Stan's slow to answer. The coffee starts to perk breaking the silence.

"Mac tells me you were looking for the airstrip. How did you know about it?"

"One night when I couldn't sleep, I found a map on your bookshelf. Thought I would check it out."

"I haven't been out there in a couple of years. Your mother keeps me in town more these days. You remind me of my younger self. You should own a gun."

"I do."

King raises his eyebrows. "Know how to use it?"

"Yes."

"We should do some target practice. Set up some bottles on a fence just like in the old Western movies. It will be fun. I haven't done that in years. Don't mention anything to the womenfolk. Don't want them to worry. It'll be wise not to mention anything to Mac when he comes. Got it?"

"Yes, sir."

King winks. "Glad we understand each other."

CHAPTER 22

I t seems that the entire county sheriff's department has arrived promptly at 8 a.m., and shortly thereafter federal agents arrive. The King dining room is transformed into a control center. A computer with an oversized screen is positioned on the table. Adjacent to the control center, King's office provides the room for interviews.

Even though Marie gave her statement yesterday to the sheriff, after reviewing video from the drone, the detective from the Drug Enforcement Agency and the FBI agent have additional questions. Both these representatives will get Stan's account of events. It is extremely intense and repetitive for the two witnesses to the point of frustration. Several moments during the process Stan needs a reminder to have patience, although he wants to scream, "I already told you." He thinks Marie is handling their questions much better. He never hears her voice loud or sounding irritated.

Stan had originally planned a couple of hours until completion; however, it soon becomes apparent that this procedure will take longer. When Jamie brings in the platter of sandwiches signaling the lunch hour, all take a much-needed break, but after the meal, the process continues.

Before leaving for work, Gabby and Brett answer questions concerning any unusual airplane activity or any strange vehicles on the roadways. After they leave, Rusty, Jamie, and the Kings are also questioned. The agents strongly request that no one discuss the matter outside the family to avoid a chance of accidentally alerting the drug lord and his men.

Finally, in the afternoon, the laptops close and the agents toss their business cards on the table and drive away, promising to provide updates on the progress of the investigation.

Marie and Stan are rocking on the chairs on the front porch with a glass of Jamie's lemonade. Marie sighs heavily and her shoulders droop.

"Pretty intense. That may have been the most questions I'd ever answered. I know they're doing their job but when Detective Harrison asked me three times in roundabout ways, speculating that I was involved, I tried my best to remain composed but inside I was annoyed." She rocks faster. "He proposed scenarios like I was intimately involved with the drug lord and that he wanted me killed because I saw something so I ran away, or perhaps the drug lord had a new squeeze and I'm jealous, so in anger I concocted the kidnapping story."

"That's terrible. I had no idea."

"Thanks, it helps when another understands. It was as if Detective Harrison was Doctor Jekyll, very kind and professional, in front of all of you, but behind closed doors with me, he was Mr. Hyde, so nasty." She shudders. "How were your interviews?"

"Pretty routine. Nothing that I didn't anticipate. They got the plane's serial number so they know the owner, and with the facial recognition software, they were able to identify two of the men. That should lead them to the others. The location of the farm is still a mystery. For the two days from the time that you escaped and until I found you, it's unclear as to the distance you traveled. It is unlikely that you ran in a straight line so they will map a two-day radius as if you walked straight and then check everything within."

"Sounds like a good plan. That's great that they're able to get all of that information from the video. Your drone came in handy." She turns away and pinches her lips tight. "They really made me feel bad."

He furls his brow. "What do you mean?"

"Like I was asking for it. That Alexa and I were irresponsible. Harrison made me feel guilty for being out at night, and for going to a bar, and dancing. He asked me about our clothing, how short our dresses were." She sticks out her lower lip. "It's like he was saying that Alexa and I are to blame." She raises her fist. "It makes me so angry." Her voice cracks and her eyes fill.

"Hey, I'm so sorry. Come here." He pulls her close. "I'm sure those questions are part of their job."

"I can't believe you are siding with them." She pushes away from his embrace.

Now he's the one who's frustrated. "Hey, hey, I'm sorry. I didn't mean for it to come across like that."

"If Alexa and I were men, do you think any of this would be relevant?"

"No. You're right. If it was me, they would not have asked. Hey, I'm sorry. We're just tired. They wore us down."

"You're probably right. I'm sorry." She reaches for his hand. "You're my hero, I won't ever forget." She sniffles. "I'm leaving tomorrow."

"What?" He shakes his head.

"Tomorrow, I fly back home...to San Diego."

Stan mumbles, "So soon?"

"My parents wanted to fly here but I convinced them it wasn't necessary and that I would come home. The detectives are finished. Now, it's a matter of them catching the bad guys, right?"

"That's my understanding."

"I'll miss this amazing place." She stands and twirls around in a full circle. "It's so peaceful and big—wide open spaces. I want to always remember this place."

"Are you too tired to look at the stars tonight?"

"Never too tired for the stars. Bring it on."

He's happy to hear her laugh. "Come on. I want to show you something else first." He takes her hand and leads her to the west side of the house. "Ryder found them this morning. The season just started. They are bluebonnets."

She kneels down and touches the periwinkle-colored blooms. "So, these are the famous Texas bluebonnets. They're beautiful."

He explains how in a week or two, the fields will be colored blue with millions of them. He tells her about other wildflowers such as the pink primrose, Indian paintbrush and the Mexican blankets. "Remind me when we go inside to show you photos. It really is incredible."

"Wow, this is awesome. I needed something positive."

"You're welcome. If you stayed, you could see how awesome it is first-hand."

She acts as though she didn't hear. He helps her stand. "Let's take a ride. I'll show you some more fields of bluebonnets on the way to the horse center. There's a field near there that's further along than these. You asked to see the center. It will be a good distraction after a tough day. You game?" He pulls on her arm. "It won't take long and I'll have you back in time for a nap before dinner. Scout's promise. Besides, you will need that nap."

"And why is that?" She furls her brow.

"Tonight, the stars will be equally as awesome, promise."

"Never too tired for the stars. But a nap would be awesome too."

CHAPTER 23

Arriving back at the ranch after their trip to the Equine Center, Marie leaves to take a nap before dinner, and Stan walks to the barn. Late morning, Rusty had taken Ryder to the neighboring ranch for a lesson in herding cattle. The Lohmans have several dogs that help with their cattle. Rusty took the initiative to ask the Lohmans to ring them when they would be moving the cattle from the winter fields to greener pastures. Rusty is a believer in learning by example. From his past experience, the easiest way to train a dog is to have another dog do the training. Ryder is the perfect breed for this work and Stan doesn't have enough fingers or toes to count the times that Rusty has mentioned training Ryder since Stan brought him home.

Stan is sad that the day of this lesson was the same day the investigators came. Once again, he's reminded that taking care of Marie and stopping this human trafficking ring takes priority. There'll be more lessons and then he will see Ryder in action.

He had some first lessons of his own while in Texas. Stan had grown up a city boy but when he first rode last spring, he loved it so much that when he returned to Washington, he continued taking lessons at a horse farm in Virginia. Always in competition with Brett, he had thought he should learn some horsemanship skills and it would be great helping King and Rusty with the ranch. Stan had watched Brett practicing his calf tie-down skills for the rodeo as well as cattle cutting. With his bum leg, he knew that calf tie-down would not be his thing so he would try cattle cutting. This important technique is used to separate a cow from the rest of the herd and very handy on a ranch.

Preparing, he studied videos on YouTube as well as having Rusty run down the basics. After his first few attempts, he was covered in dust as Texas was in a drought. And from using his legs to control the horse in those quick movements, his bad leg ached so much that he actually fell out of the saddle with his foot stuck in the stirrup. Fortunately, Rusty rescued him by stopping the horse, and he was lucky that he did not do further damage to his leg.

Reading the disappointment on Stan's face, Rusty gave him some wise and powerful advice. "Son, it's honorable that you try, and maybe in due time, you'll accomplish some of these skills, but focus your efforts on things that you do well. Things that you can be the best at doing. And, Stan, you should know, I trained many a young man and Brett is a natural. He's the best horseman. Just sayin'."

CHAPTER 24

S tan spreads the blanket on the ground before setting up the tripod for his Celestron Nexstar telescope and empties his bag with the power tank, the laser pointer, and his camera for some astrophotography. This telescope also comes with three-pointed sky alien technology, which makes it a guarantee for some phenomenal stargazing. The evening shows no signs of any advancing cloud cover and the moon is in its final waning stages. Conditions are near perfect.

He elected to set up while there was enough light, so Marie could enjoy the bluebonnets gracing this side of the hill before sunset, allowing him time to get all of the equipment readied without the use of a flashlight. Plus, this would give them quality time in a romantic setting with wine and chocolates. Stan has come well prepared.

Every time he thinks of Marie, he finds himself endlessly comparing her to Gabby. Marie is smart and feisty; Gabby is reserved and sophisticated. However, Gabby is married and Marie is single. Yep, that is the harsh reality. Gabby made her choice and it was Brett. *Move on, Stan.*

On one side of the coin, the free-spirited Stan advises him to go have some fun; enjoy life; get to know Marie; take a chance. Then, the cautious Stan on the other side of the coin kicks in—Marie's been through a lot, emotionally she's damaged; keep your distance, this isn't the right time.

He tells himself to be relaxed and the evening will take care of itself. He almost called his counselor to ask advice but then thought that silly. He's a grown man and this is simple stargazing, not a real date. Or is it?

Marie has walked a few hundred feet away to take in the flowers. After setting up his equipment, he brings out more blankets for later as the temperature drops and a pillow, as well as the cooler and his battery-operated docking station for some music. He didn't think to ask what type of music she prefers.

A short time later, Marie comes back. "It gets dark quickly."

"At this time of year, it does. But I got everything set up, just in time."

"I wish you would have let me help."

"I picked this place so you could see the field of bluebonnets. Come, sit. We can feast on champagne and chocolate-covered straw-berries."

"Seriously," she giggles. "So romantic."

He's glad that dusk hides his flushed face. He hands her a glass.

"What are we celebrating?"

"We're celebrating our success. We're celebrating your escape, good health, and also a toast in advance for the capture of the bad guys."

"And for finding Alexa." Her voice is quiet and somber.

"Yes, they'll find Alexa. I'll keep them focused. It's good you were able to access some photos off of Facebook. They will find her. We need to keep positive, right?" He touches her face, lifting her chin so he can see her eyes.

"You're right," she says in a quiet whisper.

As predicted the evening is still and cloudless. First, he easily finds Venus and Uranus, but the other planets this time of year aren't visible until close to dawn. He takes a photo of Uranus with his camera. She leans close to the telescope for a better view.

"Keep both eyes open." He stands close behind.

"I can't see anything."

"Okay, let me adjust it." He surrounds her and smells her coconut-scented shampoo. "How about now?" He accidentally touches the nape of her neck. It's soft.

"Stop," she says. He wonders if the command is directed toward his touch or if the adjustment is providing a clear image. "That's better. I can see it now. It's beautiful."

After viewing, she leans back into his chest and peers up at his face. "You're a good man, Stan."

"You hardly know me. I have my faults."

"We all do."

He moves away. "Let me show you some constellations."

Next, he sets up to view the Orion and Gemini constellations. An hour later, they take a break and lie on their backs. With his laser pointer, he points to the two stars, Castor and Pollux, the heads of the Gemini twins.

"That's the stars we just looked at."

"Tell me about them."

"That's easy. The brightest of the two is Pollux. It has an orange tint and it's the seventh brightest star in the sky."

"How far away is it?"

"About thirty-three light years."

"And the other one"

"That's Castor. It's the forty-fourth brightest star in the sky and it's about fifty light years away."

"How do you know all of this?"

"I like the stars so I study them."

He points the laser to the foot of one of the twins. "Right there will be the Eskimo Nebula. I'll put it in the telescope so you can see it. They call it the Eskimo Nebula because it resembles a head wearing a fur-lined parka."

"Really, I'll be able to see that?"

"We should."

"This is amazing."

As the night progresses, the champagne bottle empties, and she lies with her head on his chest, their conversation light. The iPod whispers country music, her choice, which surprises him a bit but she explains that the music matches the surroundings. It is Marie who props up on her elbow and peers into his face, giving him a light brush with her lips on his cheek.

"What do you want, Stan, my hero, and lover of the stars?"

He's puzzled by this question that seems to have popped out of nowhere. He stammers, "I'm not sure. I still need to figure it out."

Her laugh is contagious and when she kisses him on the lips, he eagerly responds. Her taste is sweet. He rolls her over and she's the one who grips tight around his neck, forbidding any distance between them. This closeness makes his heart beat faster.

"Thanks for sharing your stars with me." She kisses him again and this time with more passion.

Her advances and assertive moves are unfamiliar and yet intriguing. She reaches under his shirt to rub his back. He's aroused and turns to his side as her hand reaches for his crotch. "Make love to me." Her words are full of breath that warms his cheek.

Cautious Stan wants to stop but free-spirited Stan has other things in mind. It is happening fast with hormones increasing, overpowering any sanity. Their mouths hungry and their fingers caressing. In a few short minutes, he lowers her sweatpants as she unbuckles his belt. He feels the heat in his loins. Naked from the waist down, she pins him onto his back and straddles him. Moving her hips, she urges him to increase his tempo. He holds off until she muffles her screams of pleasure into his chest. Then she lies motionless, breathing deeply.

"That was unexpected, but wow." She's positioned again with her head on his chest. "You are full of surprises." He kisses her forehead and plays with her brunette locks. "Now what?"

"Explain."

"You leave in the morning."

"Yes, I go back to San Diego." Her tone flat.

"Does that mean goodbye? When will I see you again?"

"I really can't answer that because I don't know."

"Is this a one-night stand?"

"I don't know. I'm not sure."

"You asked me what I wanted a few minutes ago. I don't want this to be a one-night stand."

"Tonight, I needed to feel something. I needed to prove I was alive. Sharing the champagne and the stars with the man who rescued me. It felt right."

"It felt right to me, too. I hope this wasn't just thank-you sex."

"I'm sorry if I'm confusing you. I don't know what this means."

He thinks for a while. He should be offended, maybe angry. For him, sex between them means something. He's not going to take her answer as final. He'll persuade his case through actions, not words.

"Shhh," he says.

She starts to talk.

"Shh," he holds his finger to her lips. "I understand." He starts kissing her and his hand reaches gently between her legs.

She closes her eyes and enjoys his scent, his touch, and the weight of his body. Warm sensations tingling throughout, she gives herself to him. Currently, she may live in the moment but as time passes, she'll remember—and it's in the remembering, he hopes, that will bring her back into his arms. He'll do his best to be unforgettable.

CHAPTER 25

Early the next morning, Marie bids farewell to the King family, thanking them for their hospitality. The sheriff had offered to drive her to the airport. Stan wants the pleasure but arrangements are already made. He pulls Marie to the side as Sheriff Mac and King converse.

"You're leaving." He touches her arm.

She bites her lip. "I need to go back home. My parents wanted me to fly home yesterday."

"I'll miss you."

"I can't thank you enough." She leans in and kisses him on the cheek.

He wants more. "When will you be back?"

"Stan, I don't know. I can't think about anything as long as Alexa's life is in danger."

"You've done all you can. Now, it's up to the authorities."

"I know but I still worry."

"Call me when you land. All right?" He holds onto her hand as she steps away.

"I must go." Her voice breaks. She turns and gets into the sheriff's car and waves as it passes. He's going to miss that gal.

PART III

CHAPTER 26

King Ranch

"Y our turn," King says to Brett as he waves his rifle in the air. "Try and beat that...only missed one. I still got it." He chuckles as he wipes his gun barrel with his bandana.

Earlier that Saturday morning, with Rusty's help, King constructed a temporary firing range at the far end of the northern pasture using hay bales with paper targets attached. Some of them were typical bullseyes and others were outlines of people, which King refers to as "the bad guys." He also brought along an assortment of beer bottles and cans to align on the fence posts. He reminds Rusty, Brett, and Stan, "Not a word of this to the womenfolk. No need getting them all 'a-frettin'." He's told a white lie so that both Rita and Jamie believe that their men are going fishing for the day. It's his way to get them to prepare lunch.

Making a day of their outing, the men set up folding chairs under the shade of an old oak tree. A cooler is filled with brisket sandwiches and beer, with a bag of pork rinds with some Tabasco sauce to round out the meal. The latter is a King favorite, something he boasts that he has in common with his fellow Texan, George H.W. Bush. Later, resuming shooting, they'll make good use of the empty beer bottles.

All four men start with the idea of aiming at the bigger targets before advancing to the smaller bottles. Rusty's first to try, followed by King. Next Brett fires and afterwards shakes his head. He reports that he hasn't held a gun since his rambunctious teenage years hunting for fowl such as ducks and quail. He confesses losing bets to the other boys.

Stan patiently waits his turn. Before his motorcycle accident, he practiced at the indoor firing range weekly. In his hand he holds his Heckler & Koch Mark 23, the same gun he hid in his backpack three days ago. The cool metal object is familiar in his hand and he has great respect for its capabilities. He rubs his chin in anticipation as he's confident his skill is equal if not superior to King's.

After examining the targets and marking the previous shots, King motions for Stan to take his turn. Stan nods, reaches for his plastic goggles and takes his stand. He concentrates before he aims, then fires in slow succession at the hay bales. After six bullets, he motions for King to stand back while he reloads his gun and then after focusing for a few seconds, rapidly fires, emptying the chamber at the bottles on the fence. The breaking of glass is heard simultaneously with each shot. After his flawless performance, Stan grins and puffs out his chest like a peacock.

"Well, I'll be damned," says King. "Where'd you learn that?" He stands with his hands on his hips. "You, son, have been holdin' out on me."

"I've owned this gun for a while. What's the sense of owning a gun if you don't know how to shoot and shoot well?"

"I couldn't agree more." Rusty smiles and nods to King in approval.

Brett removes his hat. "That's pretty awesome there, Stan."

The men practice a few more rounds. Stan allows Brett to try his gun instead of the rifle and gives him a few pointers. Brett improves somewhat with practice but still can only hit an occasional bottle off the fence.

As they enjoy their picnic lunch under the tree, some rather tall tales are told by the two senior men. Most of the stories date back to their childhood experiences growing up on the ranch. Before lunch is over, Brett retreats to the car and carries back a plastic container.

"Gabby's contribution to our fishing trip," he's proud to announce.

Removing the lid, he places the container on the cooler in the circle created by their chairs.

"Chocolate chip cookies," he boasts as he shoves one into his mouth and has another in his left hand before passing the rest to Stan.

"Woohoo," King says and claps his hands. "That's my girl. Whenever she wants something, she makes chocolate chip cookies. With each bite, I wonder how much this bite is costing me." He laughs and holds his stomach. "The last time she wanted a measly million for that horse center." He chuckles again. "Brett, how much is this costing you?"

"Nothing." Brett scratches his head.

"Nothing, really?"

"Nothing that I'm aware of?" He pops the rest of the cookie into his mouth.

"You poor lovesick fool." King looks to Stan as well as Brett. "Allow me to educate you young'uns. The women went into town. So... they're going shopping. Am I right?"

"Probably." Both Brett and Stan nod in unison.

"And if you don't think that's going to run up a huge bill, you've got a lot to learn about married life."

Brett defends his position. "Gabby didn't say she needed anything."

"It's not about what she needs, it's about what she wants. Mark my words." King laughs heartily. "Women, gotta love 'em."

CHAPTER 27

ArtSmart Gallery

While the men are on their Saturday outing, the women take this opportunity to drive into town. Rita needs to tie up the final loose ends for the dinner party with the famous artist, Nicholas Templeton.

Today, the most pressing job will be hanging his artwork at the gallery. His paintings have been shipped and uncrated in the storage room. The pieces are large, each measuring between four and five feet, and are all modern canvas wrapped so they are light enough for the women to handle. Due to their size, the wall will showcase only three paintings: two square compositions and one of the larger five-by-four-foot rectangles. Rita estimates the job will take only an hour. The two additional paintings, not displayed, will be auctioned at the country club the evening of the dinner. Today, they need to decide which ones to hang and which to display on easels for the dinner.

Hanging a new show is Rita's favorite part of her job. In contrast, Gabby finds the job stressful. Rita has her finger on her chin, staring at the gallery wall where Gabby helped hang the two square Templeton pieces. Rita's deciding if the order should be reversed but elects to hang the third rectangular piece before making a final decision.

Jamie has no interest in the decision-making process and is leaving that up to the two experienced artists. This day is special as she rarely goes into town. She's browsing and stops to view Gabby's work on the adjacent wall.

"My, my, your momma would be so proud." Jamie says. "Such talent."

"Thanks," Gabby says from her perch up on the stepladder. "Rita, can you hold a little longer? This clamp won't open, it's jammed."

"I have it propped on my shoulder, but don't dawdle. Thank goodness, Nicholas isn't here. He'd go ballistic seeing his precious masterpiece teetering like this." She laughs.

"How much is this painting?"

"More than a half-year's rent. Do we have to talk about that now? Please hurry."

"Just curious. Okay, got it."

"Great, I didn't want to call your daddy and ruin his fishing trip. It's great that they all are getting out together and doing some male bonding. Hopefully after today, Stan will feel more at home here. My boy seems so distant at times, and taking off like that so far away and on his own, what was he thinking? And that poor girl. I shudder every time I think of all of the possibilities."

Gabby climbs down off the ladder, checking out the wall. "Stan's been super quiet at work. I've tried to get him to open up." She looks to Rita. "What do you think?"

"He seems better now, a bit happier after helping Marie."

"Rita, the wall...what do you think about the hanging?"

"Oh, that. I got distracted." She has her finger on her chin again. At least two minutes lapse.

"Well?" Gabby stands with her hands on her hips while waiting for an answer. Patience is not her strongest virtue.

Rita smiles. "Looks good. It's a relief to get this done. Friday will be here before we know it." She runs her fingers through her hair. "Let's reward ourselves with a nice lunch. Jamie, you in for that? Time to enjoy someone else's cooking for once. My treat."

Rita gives instructions to Lisa, the weekend clerk, and after Gabby stows the ladder, she returns to the paintings, comparing her artwork to Templeton's. His work is not only bigger in size but bolder in both color and contrast; he takes risks. Now, she's the one standing with her finger on her chin.

CHAPTER 28

Matthews Residence, King Ranch

Brett and Gabby are hanging out on their back deck enjoying the sunset, a perfect ending to their busy day as dinner ended early. She's wrapping up her fashion show, modeling some of the clothes from the shopping trip, pointing out features that follow the latest trends. His interest peaked at least ten minutes ago, but he's trying his best to stay focused.

When he was a single tennis professional, his interest in fashion was essential for charming the ladies. Back then, he prided himself on his suave look; being polished and polite brought him both women and success. He needed both to snag Gabby. Without it, he doubts if she would have given him a chance. These thoughts cause the sides of his mouth to briefly turn upward, when he thinks of their courtship. He laid everything on the line. Now he questions, has he become too comfortable?

"Brett, you aren't paying attention." Gabby pouts.

"Sorry, princess."

"What are you thinking about?"

"You, when we first met. I was thinking of you, all classy and sophisticated. How did I land such a gorgeous woman? I'm a lucky man." He takes a swig of his beer.

"Aww, that's sweet. And because you're so sweet, this one's for you." She places a box on his lap. "Open it. I hope you like it."

"If you picked it out, I'll love it. Thank you." He kisses her.

Inside the box rests a pink dress shirt. She holds it up to his face. "I knew the color was perfect for your complexion. You can wear it Friday night."

"It's pink. You want me to wear that?" He sits straight.

"It will bring out your emerald eyes. Red is opposite green on the color wheel. Trust me.

The shirt's perfect. Men who are comfortable with their manhood wear pink. You're comfortable, right?" She points with her index finger.

He stares at her in disbelief. "I don't think I've ever seen a cowboy wear pink."

She sticks out her bottom lip and twirls one of his curly locks with her finger. "You'll look super. I love a man in pink." She points at his dimple. "We haven't dressed up and been out since our wedding. We've been so busy with the ranch and the horse center. You were busy training for the rodeo. Even in December in Vegas we didn't go out. You know, really go out on the town. We used to dress nice and go to parties. I miss that."

She gives a voice to his fear that their new married life, where they decided to spend their days at the ranch, isn't enough for her.

The ranch life fulfills him in a way that his job as a tennis professional lacked. Is their honeymoon over in a short four months?

He's heard his friends express similar concerns. Their relationships seem great; then, the differences creep in. One little thing followed by another little thing, causing friction, and over time the couple drifts apart. The bliss becomes blistered. And it's a short walk from the church altar to a divorce attorney.

"We're attending a big party on Friday night. You should be excited, meeting Nicholas Templeton. Even me, the cowboy, can recite facts about Mr. Templeton."

"Oh really, is that so? Humor me." She taps her fingers on her thigh.

"What?"

"The facts about Templeton. Go ahead. I'm listening." Her eyes twinkle.

He leans back in the sofa. "What do I win?"

"Brett, why do you always need a prize? Isn't winning enough?"

"When I know I'll win, I have nothing to lose and everything to gain." He winks and holds up his beer bottle. "Okay, for starters Nicholas was a guitarist."

"That doesn't count. Give some facts about Nicholas Templeton as an artist."

"Music is an art form."

"As a painter. Give me some facts about his painting."

"Here goes—he has a worldwide reputation as one of the most exciting, contemporary, artists. His style is fresh and innovative."

"You read the brochure."

"Damn straight." He laughs and pulls her in close. "Okay, I'll wear the shirt, even if it's pink." His hand strokes her face.

"Thanks, and, Brett...you need a haircut."

"Oh, Gabby, we're moving the cattle. I don't have time to go into town."

"I can't have you looking all shaggy. The press will be there. You're a King now and we need to keep up appearances. I'll call Joni and have her drive to the ranch. Stan needs a cut as well. Rita doesn't allow my daddy to get so ragged." She flips Brett's hair off of his neck.

He rolls his eyes and is thankful that all the shopping bags are emptied.

"From all of your purchases, it seems like your day was successful."

Gabby has her feet on Brett's lap. She loves when he massages them. It makes her tingle all over. The best foreplay ever.

"We got a lot done. It was fun hanging out with Rita and Jamie. After hanging the art, we ran errands for the dinner party. I'm surprised tonight's dinner was barbecue from Cooper's instead of fish. I can't remember the last time my daddy came home from a fishing trip empty handed. No one caught anything?"

"Fish weren't biting." He looks away.

"Oh really, I'm having trouble believing that."

He grins. "But I know what is biting"—he pauses—"me." He leans toward her and nibbles on her ear.

"Stop that, you're trying to avoid the subject."

"Is it working?" His eyes gleam and his dimple deepens. He looks like a little boy itching to tell a secret that he swore to "cross my heart and hope to die" if he did.

"Something's up, Brett Matthews. I can feel it."

"I'll never tell." He playfully bites her ear again.

"Stop that."

This time he stands and picks her up from the chair, carrying her into the house. Sex is always a distraction—so much for fiction or the telling of secrets—he'll extend their honeymoon phase by keeping the flame burning.

CHAPTER 29

King Ranch

It's late, after 11 p.m. Texas time but only 9 o'clock in San Diego. Stan's phone rings.

"It's Marie. How are you?"

He perks up hearing her voice. He does miss her. "Doing well. How are you?" He sits up in the bed, propping on his pillow.

"Good, pretty good. I've been job hunting but no luck. One maybe interested, but no interviews on the books. What are you doing?"

He's not going to tell her about his day shooting. "Just stuff around the ranch. Hey, we heard from the DEA agent this afternoon. They were able to identify the other two men with the drug lord. They've also located the farm and are just waiting for the right moment, when all of them are there for a raid."

"This is great."

"They also got a lead on a prostitution ring. There's a new operation in Atlanta and he believes that Alexa may have been taken there. An undercover agent got some video inside the house and one victim resembles Alexa." He clears his throat. "I thought you would like to know. I don't want to get your hopes up, but it's encouraging."

"Thanks for that, it helps. I feel so useless sitting here doing nothing. Any news that will get her one step closer to being rescued is good news."

"If they do catch them, you'll be asked to testify. Will you be able to do that?"

"If it means a conviction and sending those monsters behind bars for life, I'll do it. I don't want another person to go through what I did. I can't even imagine what Alexa is going through."

"When are you coming to visit?"

"First, I need to get a job. I have student loans to pay."

He wants to say, *I could pay those off with one phone call,* but he doesn't. Instead he offers, "I saw some job opportunities in Texas. Have you considered looking outside of the San Diego area for employment?"

"No, after my kidnapping ordeal, the thought of leaving my family and being on my own is scary."

"I see." He's forgotten about how the situation looks from her perspective. "Have you arranged to see a counselor?"

"I am a counselor. I don't need to see one."

"Marie, you went through an extremely difficult time. The few things you told me were more than any person could handle. Now is not the time to sweep it under the rug as if it didn't happen. From my experience, denial and avoidance only makes it worse. After my motorcycle accident, I covered my feelings with pain pills and alcohol. I needed help. I couldn't do it on my own."

There is an uncomfortable silence.

"Marie..." He breathes in deeply. "Marie, I care about you. Talk to someone; if you can't do it for yourself, do it for me."

He hears sniffles and an alarm goes off. "Marie, talk to me. What's going through that pretty head of yours?" Still no answer. "Don't make me get on a plane and fly out there and drag you to therapy."

This causes her to laugh. "Stan, my hero, still trying to save me."

"This is serious."

"I am being serious. Okay, I promise to call someone in the morning."

"Thank you."

He's relieved that she promises and Marie seems to be a person who takes giving her word seriously.

Changing to a happier subject, he says, "Let me tell you about the wildflowers. The Indian paintbrush is blooming and there are a few Mexican blankets popping up..."

They chat past midnight and her final, "I miss you," is his good night lullaby.

After disconnecting with Stan, Marie hangs her head and cries. She's been so strong for so long, pretending that she's okay. Every ounce of energy has been stripped from her. She hasn't talked about it and even skirted the truth when asked by Detective Harrison. Her evasiveness caused him to come to the wrong conclusion that she must have been involved with Lopez and his organization. The memories are so painful that by pushing them back into the far corners of her mind, she attempts to erase them as if they never happened.

She's done a fairly good job at this until the darkness obscures the light. At night, unable to sleep, she tosses and turns relentlessly and if she does doze off, is haunted by nightmares that awaken her in cold sweats. Some of these visions are cloudy, and she has a hard time separating the facts of what happened to her in the grip of the kidnappers from some movie scenes or from the stories her patients have shared. There are large gaps in her recall, probably from shock, or denial and disbelief; however, filling in those gaps takes second place to the biofeedback exercises she has resorted to, attempting to slow her fast, racing heart. Yes, it is exhausting.

Lately these panic attacks are happening more frequently and sometimes she reverts to sitting huddled on the floor, rocking back and forth with her head between her hands. At these times she silently whispers repeatedly, "You're safe now...take slow deep breaths... you're okay. Slow down, heart... you're safe. It's okay...you escaped... you're free."

She's tried some self-hypnosis techniques but whenever she gets uncomfortable, she's distracted and her memory skips to another scene. It's as though she were watching a movie and then left the theater for a popcorn run and came back oblivious to the action on the big screen.

In her profession, a patient's mind does this during extreme trauma as a way of protection since what's too painful to remember, one chooses to forget. Without question, if a patient came to her with these symptoms, she would suggest therapy, including hypnotherapy and support groups. But she doesn't wish to share her experience for fear of upsetting her friends and family. She chooses to stand alone.

As a witness, during the trial, she'll be asked to recall every detail. If she uses the excuse that she can't remember, the court will discard her testimony. What good is a witness who cannot give details?

She's tried journaling but she can't concentrate and is easily distracted. However, looking back with a psychologist mindset, in her short time at the ranch and with Stan, she was in denial. She told herself a lie. She told herself that she was brave and strong. Sadly, instead she was weak and frail and she leaned on him. When they were together, he was her strength. He was her hero and her savior. She believes without his help, she would have died lying there on the ground.

Reminded of her connection with Stan, she regains some emotional balance. It was important to feel close to him and having sex with him gave her a sense of self-worth, gratitude, and also control. Perhaps her dependence on him is unhealthy and unfair, which is a bothersome concept. He deserves better.

CHAPTER 30

King Ranch

Yo, Pablo here. I need to speak to the boss ...It's none of yo' business. He tol' me to talk directly to 'im. I'll wait. Tell 'im I'm on the line."

A few minutes later Eugene Lopez is connected. "Well, Pablo, my friend."

"Hey, boss. Funny stuff goin' round here. Thought you should know."

"Tell me."

"I hear all this shootin' and I'm thinkin' what the hell is that? So I go and check it out, you know...like you told me, keep an eye on things. The men are out there just firin' up the place."

"Explain that, firing up the place."

"They got these here rifles and guns and stuff and they got some targets. It's like they're practicing for somethin'. In the years I work here, never seen nothin' like it. I wouldn't thought nothin' much 'bout it 'cept the sheriff was here again—that's the third time. Another time, since I called you last. Sheriff never comes here like that. And some other car, looked official but I don't know, some guy dressed up like a bigwig of some kind got out. Oh, and then there was that senator, Senator Wright, tall guy. You know, Richard Wright."

"Oh yes, Senator Wright. He and King have always been tight. I may have to pay our good senator a visit. And the Jeep..."

"Yep, it's black, dirty as all get-out but black. I wiped off the dirt to be sure. Yep, it's black."

"What about the girl?"

"She was stayin' at the daughter's place but I haven't been over there. Pretty sure, she's there."

"Good job, Pablo. Expect something, a bonus. More where that comes from. And, Pablo, find out more about the girl."

"I'll do my best but don't wanna be askin' too many questions."

"Pablo, the girl, just do it."

"Yes, sir, boss. You can count on me."

"Good."

The line is disconnected.

Pablo has worked on the ranch for over two years. He usually stays in the bunk house on weekends, as he has no family other than some distant cousins who live south of Nuevo Laredo. Twice a month on payday, he hitches a ride to the nearest bar to drink and shoot darts with the other wranglers. Some out-of-towners were passing through a few months ago, and after learning he worked for Wayne King, they gave him a cell phone and offered him money. All he has to do is call in every so often and give a report.

Ain't nothing illegal; it ain't hurtin' anyone, Pablo thinks. He's like a news reporter like he sees on the TV behind the bar.

CHAPTER 31

Country Club / ArtSmart Gallery

The ballroom is buzzing. The orchestra plays an assortment of classical music including Beethoven, Chopin and Debussy. Templeton requested the latter as he feels Debussy's impressionistic compositions parallel the vision he portrays in his artwork.

The tables are eloquently set, adorned with candles and large floral arrangements. The Valentine holiday near, the theme follows the same using reds, whites and pinks. King, Rita, and Nicholas stand at the doorway greeting attendees. King's black suit pales next to Nicholas' eccentric untucked purple silk shirt and geometric print pants. It's as if the artist is a blinking neon light against a black background. Rita, wearing dark pink, tea-length chiffon, smiles and stands back allowing King to take the lead introducing the artist.

Framing the front podium are two of Templeton's masterpieces. King bought them already and plans to auction them for charity. The nonprofit, Art for Young Artists, will receive the proceeds from the first painting and the EAT Program will benefit from the second.

Most of the VIPs have arrived—the governor and the first lady, Senator Wright, and House representatives from the local districts, as well as many company CEOs and partners from major law firms. King's a great facilitator, and his priority for this dinner is not about promoting art or raising funds for charities but about getting enough votes to pass his bill in the state legislature. Templeton's art and the charities are the means to the end.

Gabby arrived in town earlier this morning so she could have her hair styled at the salon. Since she continues to own her condo off Congress, she and Brett will stay overnight. This week preparing for Templeton's visit, she's aware that since their marriage, last October, they have become boring homebodies. In the future, they really should make better use of the condo by spending weekends here enjoying dinner, the theater, and the symphony. She'll propose her idea to Brett.

She glances around the room searching for him. He's hitching a ride with Stan and they're late.

Minutes later, standing speaking with her daddy's poker buddies, Gabby excuses herself from the group as she sees Brett walking toward her. Crossing the room, she observes as a group of women stop Brett, creating a circle around him. She relives images of his days working at the country club. He was a popular tennis pro and women vied for his attention. Watching his frequent gestures with his hands, she notices the light catching his wedding band and she smiles. The ring confirms that he's taken and her heart swells. He must sense her closeness and returns her smile. As he leaves the group, one of the women grabs Brett's arm, firm enough for him to halt. This action fires up a jealous streak and Gabby's quick to approach.

"Brett, there you are, my daddy needs you. Excuse us." She flashes a smile and pulls him away.

"Thanks for the rescue." He scans her from head to toe. "You look great. I like your hair. The first night we danced, your hair was up."

"You remember."

He reaches over and touches a curl. "Of course, I remember everything." He leans in and gives her cheek a quick brush and whispers, "Later, I'd like a repeat." His eyes twinkle.

"You just walked through the door and you're dazzling the ladies with those green eyes and that pink shirt. I told you it was a winning combination. You look perfect, Brett Matthews."

"I have a personal shopper. I'll tell her you approve." They walk toward the bar. He hands her a glass of chardonnay and keeps the bourbon. "So that's the famous Nicholas Templeton. Who's his personal shopper?" He takes a sip from his glass. "Thank you for not buying that outfit. I'll never complain about a pink shirt."

"Where's Stan? He gave you a ride, right? I don't see him."

"Yes, we rode together. I don't know; there's so many people here. Can I help? What's up?"

"It's probably nothing but a few minutes ago, Mr. Lopez asked for an introduction. It's odd."

"Why is that? Who's this Mr. Lopez?"

"He's standing over there." She nods over her shoulder. "The older, distinguished-looking man with the mustache in that group behind me. He owns several companies. My daddy's not his friend; the men have had their differences. However, he's very influential and has a stake in the oil bill passing. I wonder why he wants to meet Stan."

"Enough about Stan. The music calls, let's dance." He bows and she curtsies, offering her hand.

After the dinner and auction, the evening progresses from the country club ballroom to the art gallery. The ballroom had been dimly lit with a romantic ambience, in contrast to the art gallery that is bright and alive with conversation. Rita had the staff move a few of the table floral arrangements to the gallery and place several arrangements together in large floor urns of different sizes. The idea proved genius; the gallery looks highly professional and elegant at the same time. Artist Templeton is animated and holding the crowd's interest as he explains his art, and immediately two labels acquire red stickers before dessert is served.

Gabby mingles near her artwork, chatting with guests who browse the gallery, when from behind a deep voice asks, "Which is your favorite?"

She jumps at his closeness.

"Sorry for startling a beautiful artist." Eugene Lopez kisses her hand, then turns to admire her art. "The one on the top left is as if angel wings are touching elements of nature, so light that if not paying attention, it could be overlooked."

His warm breath on the nape of her neck raises goosebumps. "However, the one beneath hides something. Intriguing, see how the darker purple hovers over the hues of blue." He sips his champagne.

"I love champagne. My apologies." He grabs a glass from the passing waiter's tray.

"Thank you, but I've had my limit tonight."

"Please share in a toast." He hands her the glass and his touch lingers on her fingers. "The least you can do for a man who admires and understands your work. Consider these two sold."

She stammers, "Thank you," and lifts her glass in unison, looking deep into his shifty eyes in an effort to read what lies behind the brown beads.

"You've yet to introduce me to Stan, your stepbrother. I understand he's come upon some hard times."

"Stan's doing fine." She studies this man's face and finds him audacious, leaving her unsettled.

"Senator Wright, my personal friend...oh, yes, the two of you were together, when we first met. The senator has been in close contact with the authorities, and then so is Stan, from what I understand."

Steady, Gabby, this man is baiting you. He is fishing with these tidbits of unrelated topics, clearly having nothing to do with the events of the evening.

She lowers her eyes and forces a composed reply. "I'm not sure what you are getting at, Mr. Lopez. A smart woman refrains from knowledge of men's affairs. I cannot help you."

"Please, call me Eugene. I would like to be on a first-name basis with such a beautiful and talented artist."

"Eugene, my daddy can address all your concerns. Let's find him."

"No need to bother him about such things on this remarkable evening. My dear, I have great respect for your father."

"As do I. Thank you for coming tonight and for your support. I will have the paintings delivered to your office Monday."

He nods his head as she turns away from him in one swift motion as if on a pressing mission.

An hour later the crowd wanes. Gabby and Brett are sitting on the couch in the back room.

Stan enters. "Mind if I join?" He rubs his leg.

"Is everyone gone?" Gabby asks.

"Almost, the last couple is having a heart-to-heart conversation with my mother and your dad. I think this was a success. What's your take?"

"The art sold. Nicholas was magical. He's quite a salesman. I don't have that skill."

"Gabby, you sold paintings as well."

"Speaking of that, the buyer is Mr. Lopez. He's creepy."

Brett sits straighter. "What do you mean?"

"Stan, do you know him?" Gabby says.

"No, should I?"

"He asked me twice to introduce you. He mentioned the authorities talking to Richard and in the same sentence mentioned you as well."

"Do you think Richard told him anything? We were given strict instructions not to discuss it with anyone." Brett shakes his head.

"Which guy was he?" Stan says.

Brett gets out his phone. "Let's Google him. Gab, what's his first name?"

Gabby says, "That's easy. He made a point of asking me to call him Eugene...Eugene Lopez. He's an oilman."

Brett pulls up Lopez's profile online. There are many photos and business articles referring to his oil company and some other industrial businesses. Brett shares the photos of Eugene Lopez with Stan and his eyes widen.

"What is it? Do you recognize him?" Brett asks.

Stan rubs his forehead. "I can't be certain, but he looks like one of the guys on the video."

They all stare at each other as if in disbelief.

Stan is the first to break the silence. "If he knows we are on to him, Marie could be in danger. I need to alert her and quick." He stands and takes his cell phone from his pocket.

"Stan, wait. Let's talk to Daddy and get the proper authorities involved."

"They don't care about Marie. I need to warn her." Stan paces around the small back room.

Brett stands and confronts Stan. "You'll scare the poor girl. Then what? What's your plan? You're in Texas, she's in California. Let the authorities protect her."

Gabby rubs Stan's back. "Brett's right. Let's tell Daddy and together we'll make a plan, a good plan that will help Marie."

CHAPTER 32

Downtown

The following afternoon, the task force assembles in a conference room at the state capitol arranged by Senator Wright. The King family is joined by the DEA and the FBI. Sheriff Mac is absent. After learning of Gabby's exchange with Lopez, there is concern that he's been warned and their original plans may need to be expedited. The DEA and the FBI already had identified Lopez as the drug lord from the drone footage but felt it wise to release as little information as possible to help keep the lid on things until they made the arrest.

Each person is interviewed separately in hopes of discovering how information could have been leaked. Rusty and Jamie are interviewed by Sheriff Mac back at the ranch and join the others via video conferencing. Everyone swears that they maintained silence. Still, the possibility remains that Stan's Jeep was seen by the pilot when he flew the plane low overhead after taking off, and the pilot might have come to an obvious conclusion—that King's aware that someone is trespassing on his land and using the airstrip. But this is not sufficient proof that these men are involved in the marijuana farm and human trafficking. After all the interviews are finished, the conclusion from the team is Marie is the sole witness to the farm and the kidnappers. Stan had paced back and forth; he needed to be Marie's advocate.

Developing a new plan of action is essential. The fear arises that Lopez will—or already has—shut down operations. Then finding Alexa would be nearly impossible. As a precaution, since Marie's capturers have her driver's license with her California address, Marie will be placed into the witness protection program.

Everything needs to be expedited, creating a whirlwind of activity. All are to keep vigilant and notify authorities of any unusual activity; however, the Kings are instructed to carry on daily life as normal.

CHAPTER 33

King Ranch

Normal duties will go forward. It's Monday morning and the day the wranglers are to move the last of the cattle to the spring pastures. The sun won't grace the horizon for another couple of hours, but Jamie circles the table pouring steaming coffee into the men's mugs.

King says, "Stan, I got a call from Detective Harrison, and Marie will be picked up this morning. He asked that there be no communication. I told them that it won't be a problem." His face shows serious concern as he speaks. "I know you have feelings but now is the time for restraint. I'm also aware that you have resources. Son, don't do anything stupid. I don't mean to be harsh but all of our actions could mean the difference between life and death. I need your word."

Stan swallows hard, matches King's stare. "Yes, sir," he answers and quickly turns to hide his disappointment. He had wanted to have at least one more talk with Marie before the weeks of silence.

Next, King addresses Brett and Rusty. "Limit phone conversation to ranch activities. To stop talking altogether would raise a red flag so call as you normally would; just limit the topics of conversation." He raises his coffee mug. "Today, we're all together. Besides, it's days like today that put a smile on this old man's face. Nothing I enjoy more than serenading a herd of cattle into greener pastures."

Rusty says, "Lohman's man is coming with his dog. Ryder's done great with his training but for this time, Butch will be here as Ryder still needs to learn the commands—'away to me' for right and 'come by' for left. Ryder can show us what he's learned."

Brett smiles. "He's a smart dog. Stan, will you be riding?"

"I plan on it."

"You can take the Jeep if your leg is bothering you."

Stan rolls his eyes. Why does it always come down to his leg?

Rusty pats Stan on the back. "Ryder's not the only one who's been training. Stan's done real good out there. I think you men will be surprised."

"Good for you, Stan. With Stan's help and Ryder, Brett here, and of course Rusty, what more can a guy need?" King picks up a slice of bacon and pops it into his mouth.

"A man, and all his friends, need lunch," Jamie says with a chuckle. "Exactly where? Not one of you have mentioned which pasture. I don't read minds. Well...sometimes I do." She winks.

"Rusty, you didn't tell your woman, shame."

Rusty swats Jamie on the hind side as she rounds the table. "Rusty, stop that. I'll take my rolling pin after you."

"Can we video that? I would like to use it as training. Teach these young fellows here what happens when you let the womenfolk take over." He sits back in his chair. "Women allow men to believe that the men are in charge but any married man will tell you, that ain't the way it is." They all laugh.

"The north pasture is where we'll be headed. See you there before noon if you can. The guys will need a break."

CHAPTER 34

Matthews House

G abby hears the alarm beep to awaken Brett and then goes back to sleep. Brett will be in good hands as Jamie serves a hearty breakfast. He loves ranching as much as her daddy, but today will be a tiring day. He'll come home dusty from head to toe, but he'll have a wide smile and anxious to share stories.

She's using this opportunity to sleep in. She loves Brett dearly but will also enjoy her alone time. However, since it will take the wranglers till almost noon to get the cattle halfway, she can join them for the drive the last few hours. It's always a thrill to watch Brett and her daddy in action and Lady, her horse, needs exercise.

As a young girl, as often as allowed, she rode at her daddy's side. It was something they shared and now Brett shares this with them. Caught in daydreaming, the sound of a truck in the driveway brings her to the present. *That's strange—did Brett forget something?*

She peeks out the window and watches three strange men hop out of the black vehicle. Their walk is purposeful and two hold guns.

Her heart leaps, reacting to her intuition that tells her that this is not a neighborly visit. These men mean business. There are no local roads that come by her house. The only drive is by the main house and surely Rita or Jamie would have called. These men must have driven across the prairie and grasslands. But why?

Texas frequently has tornado warnings and a fair number of touchdowns, so she included a safety shelter when designing the house. Thinking fast, she pushes the button that slides the bookcase revealing the opening to the shelter. She crawls in and slides the bookcase back into place. Her heart beats like thunder on her eardrum, and she fears they will hear. Thankfully she remembers to silence her cell. Moving to the far corner, she kneels, placing her hand over her mouth. She wills herself to take slow deep breaths in an effort to keep her from spiraling out of control.

The sound of breaking glass, followed by loud voices, makes her tremble uncontrollably. These men are dangerous. Their footsteps mimic her beating heart and they are close. She lowers her eyes and prays.

Their words are muffled but she can hear enough to fill in the gaps.

"Look everywhere."

"Check the guest rooms. Pablo said she was staying here."

She hears heavy footsteps. It occurs to her that these men must be looking for Marie.

"There's no sign of her. Nothing. The guest room is empty. No clothes. Nothing in the bathroom to indicate that someone's been here."

"Or maybe she's gone. Maybe Pablo didn't know what he was talking about."

"This bed is still warm. The King woman can't be too far. "

"I'll alert the boss."

He talks on his phone. "Hey, boss...nothing. We're here at the Matthews house. Nothing, no girl. No Ms. King. House is empty." There's a pause. "Yep, they're moving the cattle, like he said. Want us to go to the main house?"

"Boss says to make it look like a robbery. Don't leave any fingerprints. If we find the King woman, we're to take her instead. Go check the garage."

Gabby's eyes get wider. *What do they want with me?*

Next Gabby hears the toppling over of furniture and opening of drawers, more glass breaking, and she moves her hands to cover her ears to stifle the noise.

She cowers in the safety shelter long after the voices are gone and the sound of the truck leaving. She takes no chances.

Hours later, the need to go to the bathroom is motivation to leave the shelter. Her cell is worthless inside here, as the cement walls block any chance of getting a signal. For the future, she'll put a gun in here and perhaps a bucket and TP. In all her thoughts, she's never envisioned her shelter as a hiding place. In all of the stories that were told by her grandparents and great-grandparents, there was never an intruder, let alone a group of dangerous men with an evil purpose.

After dialing Sheriff Mac with trembling fingers, the time to be brave passes and her plans for the afternoon are derailed. Gabby buckles over and cries.

Now, that she's had her cry, she retrieves her gun from the locked wooden cabinet and the bullets from her desk and loads it. Damn, she's a King and she better start acting like it. Let them come back, she'll be ready.

CHAPTER 35

Today is the second day of the cattle drive started on Saturday to cover the forty miles between the winter and spring pastures. With the rains, this pasture was chosen because the creeks run freely and the grass tall. Rusty and King planned a two-day drive to prevent the cattle from losing weight, which could make them too thin to take to market in a few weeks. To ensure an easy drive for both the men and the cattle, every cowboy has a job. King and Rusty ride in the front; as leaders they set the pace. They're also responsible for talking and singing as singing has a calming effect on the cattle. The two men have worked side by side, chanting the same folk songs and ditties for nearly four decades.

The other men have their assigned tasks to ensure a successful drive. Brett and another wrangler are the flank riders. They manage the sides, keeping the herd in a compact group. Finally, Stan, with the help of Pablo, takes up the rear; they are the drag riders. The whole process is new to Stan and he's excited to be included in this ritual.

Later in the afternoon, Stan sits high in the saddle surveying the pasture. It's been a challenge but he's kept up with this team. And he's not the only one doing a good job; he's very proud of Ryder. Rusty's hours of training are evident. In addition to teaching the canine the basic commands of herding, on several occasions Rusty had brought a few cattle into the corral so Ryder could get familiar with the cows. During these lessons, Ryder was taught how to respond to a whistle command and a few hand gestures. The neighbor's dog, Butch, has been great at sharing with Ryder how to maintain eye control combined with the "clap down" technique to give a predatory look that the cattle respect. These techniques seem to be instinctive as Ryder has mastered the skills quickly.

In the early morning on the drive, Ryder paired with Butch but after lunch, Ryder and Stan have become a pair, at the back of the herd. Ryder's bark seems to get the cattle moving. He still has much to learn, but he knows the herd needs to follow the leader in a group and he's good at nipping the cows on their ankles if his bark isn't enough to get them to stop grazing and to continue forward. Stan enjoys a feeling of comradery, not only from the feeling of duty to attain a common goal with the men, but he's also experiencing a connection with Mother Nature. Watching Ryder from a distance, Stan's uncertain if it's he or Ryder who's enjoying this work the most. The borador jumps and runs in ways Stan has never seen in the past.

It's late afternoon when the gate to the pasture is closed, a signal that the work's completed. Now, the men leisurely ride back to the barn. They relate stories of the day and Stan actually feels he's a part of this brotherhood for the first time since he's been at the ranch.

As they near the barn, a police car in the drive is a sign that there's new development in the investigation. Perhaps Lopez has been arrested. However, as of yesterday, there still wasn't enough evidence to arrest him on the human trafficking charges. Rusty takes the horses and shoos King, Brett, and Stan toward the house. Their relaxed mood is abandoned.

CHAPTER 36

Matthews Home Later That Evening

Gabby parts the curtain and stares at the police car in the driveway. It's past ten o'clock and she should be brushing her hair. It's a bedtime ritual that her mother started so they could talk and even in these years since Anna passed, Gabby still upholds the tradition. Many serious life topics were discussed during this time; however, the matters about relationships and love are the most memorable. But tonight, the practice is replaced by concern for their safety. Perhaps she and Brett should have taken Sheriff Mac's advice and driven into town for a few days. On the other hand, Detective Harrison advised them to stay. Is he hoping that Lopez will chance a second attempt? Gabby feels that unlikely and even reckless. Lopez may be creepy and arrogant, not stupid.

It's clear she doesn't understand their strategy. The detective saw no need to interview Pablo. It's as if he didn't trust her account of the events or what she'd heard. At times, it seems that the agencies know more than they're willing to share with the King family.

Gabby thinks that's easy for them as their goal is to collect enough evidence to convict; their goal doesn't seem to take into account the human lives that could suffer from this waiting game, especially the danger it presents to the Kings. What if she didn't have the tornado shelter? What if they took her hostage? Look what they did to her house. She's not going to sleep tonight.

Today, it took hours for the detectives to gather evidence: fingerprints, footprints, and tire tracks. They took hundreds of photos. She was forbidden to touch anything, and sitting here in the disheveled mess caused her insides to cringe. Again, and again, and again, she was asked to give an account of the events. It happened so fast she's confused as to the repetition of the questioning. It was as if they were trying to discredit her story. Her stomach kept doing flip-flops. She might have had some satisfaction if she could have vomited on Detective Harrison's polished Bally shoes. The more she went over the details, the more her dislike for him deepened.

She closes her eyes and hangs her head. He couldn't understand how she didn't know the make and model of the truck, why she didn't get the license plate number or why she was so sketchy describing the men. "For God's sake, there were only three," she recalls Harrison screaming. She shudders. She had held her ground and she didn't cry. He makes her so angry—it's as if she's the one on trial. She recalls Marie describing similar complaints. Maybe Harrison has a thing against women.

Now, Brett stands behind her and places his arms around her waist. She leans back into his bare chest.

"They're going to be there all night."

"I know."

He hugs a little tighter. "I'm so sorry. You were smart to remember the storm shelter."

"I'm sorry I didn't have my gun. I would have shot them." Her voice is determined. She's thankful he can't see her eyes as he would have seen hardness that teeters on the edge of hate. She hopes he never sees this part of her.

"Gabby, there were three men. You may have gotten off one shot, but three against one, you did the right thing."

"It doesn't feel like the right thing. It feels wrong. It feels like they won."

He turns her to face him. "They aren't winning. This move today was a move of desperation. They're scrambling. The detectives want all of them...they want the drugs, and the human trafficking. Being patient will bring down the entire operation. They need time to find Alexa and all of the other women and children. Patience, princess. The whole department has made this a priority."

"And in the meantime?"

"In the meantime, we'll carry on as normal." He closes the curtain. "Come with me to bed and let's forget about the officers and forget about Detective Harrison. It'll be just you and me." He brushes her hair away from her face.

"The only reason the officers are here is because Daddy insisted. Harrison wasn't going to give us any protection at all. We're got plywood over the broken windows, for God's sake. I don't trust him. What if he's dirty—you know, like in the movies. He's really in cahoots with Lopez and he's going through the motions but not really doing anything."

"Hey, hey, you have watched too many television shows." He kisses her on the top of her head.

"I'm sorry. I'm so angry and I feel so helpless." Her guard lowers and her eyes fill with tears.

"It's okay, really it's okay. We're going to get through this." He leads her away from the window.

"I'm sorry you missed the cattle drive today. I love to see you ride. Let's pack a picnic lunch and ride tomorrow. Let's try to forget all about this."

"I'd like that." She turns one last time toward the window and offers a prayer.

CHAPTER 37

King Ranch House

Gabby's not the only member of the King clan looking out the window, and tonight it's not the stars that lure Stan. *How can anyone possibly sleep?* The conversation at the dinner table and the one later, after Gabby and Brett left, swirl around in his mind. In the latter, with Gabby out of earshot, King spoke his mind. His manner was completely opposite of the calm, matter-of-fact demeanor that he presented before, and it took them all by surprise.

Stan has never seen King this angry; he recalls the conversation with precision. King faulted the FBI for the lack of surveillance. They should have been aware that Lopez's men were on the move, and the thought that they were on his property, threatening his daughter, makes his blood curdle. Stan saw his mother jump as King slammed his fist on the table. The room remained silent for an uncomfortable period of time following his outrage.

Earlier, Harrison had also refused to share any information as to the progress of the investigation. There was no timeline revealed and they were told to sit tight and let the authorities do their job. Yes, it was King's insistence with Harrison, followed by a subsequent phone call, that got security guards at Gabby's house tonight. Detective Harrison didn't seem to think that the situation warranted such efforts.

Stan firmly believes that King's current respect wasn't obtained by sitting back and waiting for others. In his eyes, King is proactive and firmly believes that God helps those who help themselves. With his trust in the authorities shattering, Stan is convinced King will prevent another incident such as this happening on his watch.

CHAPTER 38

Matthews Home the Next Morning

"Gabby, we should go." Brett calls from the kitchen. He opens the side door and waves to the officers as they are changing shifts. The sun is shining bright and there isn't a cloud in the sky and the birds are singing.

"You go on ahead. I'll walk, I need the exercise," she answers from the bedroom.

"Gab, you know that's not going to happen. Come on." He rinses his coffee cup in the sink.

He walks down the hall and stands in the doorway of their bedroom. She's dressed but still brushing her hair. "Hey, princess, I'm late. Can you do that there?"

"Brett, go on. I'll be fine."

"Your dad will have my hide. You know that. Please..."

The defeated tone of his voice gets her to stand, walk over to him. She wraps her arms around his neck.

"Okay, for you, dear, I'll go over but I'm coming back."

"We talked about going riding, remember."

"That was before."

"Before what?"

"Before Rusty has you off doing whatever it is that you're supposed to do out there." She waves her hand in the air.

"Corral a few cows that got out through a downed fence. It won't take long. I'll be back before you're finished packing our picnic lunch. Deal?"

She twitches her nose and leaves to grab her hat.

"Work with me here, Gab."

"You weren't here. They came into our home. They broke the windows. They turned over furniture, emptied drawers. And that Harrison guy, he's worthless, he doesn't care one bit about us. All he wants is credit for busting that human trafficking ring. He wants his gold star, his minutes of fame. In a split second, he expected me to get a license plate number, and be able to describe three guys with guns. He acts like he can't do his job because I failed to spoon-feed him all the information. What is he doing, Brett? How is he helping?"

"Gab, we talked about this. Our hands are tied. Do we have to start our day talking about this again?"

"It makes me so angry."

"I can see that. But regardless, we need to go. Rusty has texted me twice. Please hurry. I'll be in the car."

After he's out of sight, Gabby opens her nightstand and retrieves her gun. Rolling the ivory handle over in her hands, she recalls the first time she held it. Her parents gave her this gun on her eighteenth birthday.

"Happy birthday, sweetheart." Her parents came into the living

room together carrying a package. She remembers the shine as light hit the foil wrapping and the large bow. Ripping the paper, then opening the box, she was stunned. She had seen the gun before her only once and that was more than a decade ago. She was around five years old as she wasn't yet enrolled in school and her mother was in the study, kneeling in front of an opened gun case. Unaware that Gabby had slipped into the study, Anna held a small handgun, turning the ivory handled grip over in her hands. The pistol was dark silver and had a bluish sheen and Gabby thought it pretty.

Here on her birthday, her daddy breaks the silence. "Now that you turned eighteen, your mother and I want you to have your grand-mother's Smith and Wesson. We'll go out when you're ready and I'll teach you how to shoot, but first you need to learn how to care for it and most of all learn to have respect for what it can do."

"Yes, Daddy," she answered as she turned the ivory handle grip in her hands as she saw her mother do all those years ago.

Several weekends following her birthday, King taught her how to clean, load and unload, and to shoot. At first, she was afraid of the gun, but eventually she felt more comfortable and even enjoyed going out and shooting targets that King assembled. She was never a great shot, but she could manage.

In the decade that has followed, Gabby never felt a need to use the gun or even practice shooting. However, she has routinely cleaned it once a year around her birthday. But today, after yesterday's ordeal, she feels vulnerable and she has a need; placing the gun in her back-pack, she'll be ready. A King is always prepared.

CHAPTER 39

King Ranch House

With Brett gone to work with Rusty and her dad, she has idle time on her hands. Gabby sets up her easel in the corner by the window, a familiar setting as it is where she's painted for nearly two decades. In the past, she has used painting to work through emotions and to find answers. The terrifying events yesterday created lingering insecurity along with frustration that has quickly turned from anger to rage toward Detective Harrison. She deems his decisions lacking, and the use of badgering techniques in questioning leaves her feeling inadequate. How can she paint? But for her heart to heal she's convinced that painting will put this entire mess into perspective.

Her initial urge to brush black paint all over her canvas wanes after the first strokes of the brush and now she stands back. From her observation the composition looks as though a black hole has swallowed the brighter colors in its path. Disturbed, she tries to diminish the intensity of the black, wiping it away with a cloth before it dries.

The black paint smears and soon it is on her hands and apron. The canvas is a mess and she's one as well. She throws her hands up in the air. *It's impossible for me to paint. What was I thinking?* She turns away, defeated, and cleans the mess. Forcing the issue has never achieved good results. Painting will have to wait for a calmer heart.

An hour later, the picnic lunch is packed and Gabby's waiting for Brett to return.

Rita's phone rings and after seeing the caller on the screen, she puts the phone on speaker. Gabby perks up hearing her best friend's voice.

"Ella, hello, how are you, girlfriend?"

"Gabby, this is a nice surprise. I get you and Rita with one call."

Rita asks, "How's the baby?"

"All's going well. Had a check-up this morning. Baby's heart rate is good. I'm getting so fat. I'm not even going to tell how much weight I've gained. Will thinks I look great. But my feet have started to swell and my blood pressure is up a bit. And this little girl has been kicking away. If all this continues, I'll need to stop work. I put my papers in asking for leave starting the end of the month. But enough about me, how are things there?"

Gabby gives Rita the quiet sign with her index finger to her lip. It makes no sense to worry Ella about all of their recent drama.

Rita agrees, keeping with the unspoken gesture. "All is great here as well. The bluebonnets are out."

"I miss Texas, especially this time of year with all of the wild-flowers. It's so beautiful there. No flowers here. Quite the opposite as we had some snow flurries just yesterday."

"When you quit working, maybe you can come here and stay to deliver your baby so that Texas is on the birth certificate."

"My parents would love that. She would be a fifth-generation Texan. Will doesn't quite understand the importance." She giggles. "I have yet to convert that man."

"Have you picked a name?" Rita asks. "And just to let you know, I'm knitting pink booties."

"I didn't know you could knit."

"My dear, I am full of surprises. Just wait until I can get my hands on my granddaughter." She smiles. "A name?"

"No, not yet. Will and I are tossing around a few but we haven't decided. Any suggestion from either of you?"

"Will's grandmother's name was Laura. That's a nice name for a sweet baby girl," says Rita.

"Thanks, I'll put it on the list. If you want us to consider any others, text me. Changing the subject, Will misses having his brother close. Has Stan decided if he's staying on the ranch?"

Rita speaks up first. "His condo is rented until the end of the summer. I think he's enjoying Texas. He went out on the cattle drive yesterday and came back excited. Plus, he seems to like his job at the horse center. Gabby can speak to that better than I can."

Gabby says, "He's doing a really great job at the center. As far as living here permanently, he seems to change his mind daily—some days he talks about staying and the next, he talks about returning to DC. It's hard to tell."

The conversation with Ella proves to be a good stress releaser and it makes the time pass faster, as it has taken Brett and her daddy longer than expected to round up the cattle and get them back to the pasture. When he kissed her goodbye, Brett mentioned that it would only take an hour and it has been more than a couple.

Gabby was grateful that Ella didn't question why she wasn't at the Equine Center. Stan has been managing the place and the therapist offered to help. Gabby agreed with Brett that she should take time off, although their reasons differ as to why.

After the call with Ella, Gabby's restless. From her experience, her daddy isn't going to stop looking until he found every one of those missing cattle. Much like the biblical story that tells of the shepherd leaving the ninety-nine to look for the one lost sheep. Brett is not one to suggest to her daddy when to quit a search. Their afternoon picnic and ride through the ranch is getting shorter by the minute. Time for Plan B.

Gabby says her goodbyes to Rita, grabs her backpack and her picnic basket. She walks toward the barn, saddles up Lady and straps the basket to the saddle. Then she goes out to the garden where Jamie is gathering lettuce, spring onions, and dandelions for tonight's dinner.

"You still here?" Jamie stands up, places her hand on her lower back and wipes the sweat from her brow.

"Here, let me do that." Jamie hands her the knife and Gabby pulls a spring onion out of the ground and cuts off the top.

Watching her peel the outer skin removing the dirt, Jamie says. "Your mother loved the first onions of the season. I miss her. I surely do miss her. I think of her a lot when I'm here in the garden. It was one of her favorite places."

Gabby puts her arm on the older woman's shoulder. "I miss her too. She's been gone a while now."

"Ten years, next week." Jamie turns away. "But who's counting? Life goes on. Some days I only think of her once or twice, other days it's different. Those days seems like every little thing brings her to mind. Anna loved this land. Rita's nice but she's not your momma. Your momma and I were like sisters." She crosses her fingers together. "Just like this. We had so much fun together. She was way too young...damn cancer."

"She did love the ranch, and she loved you as well. All three of us would plant this garden, weed it, water it, and then harvest it. Nothing made us happier than taking off our shoes so we could feel the fresh ground between our toes. And then, after supper, we would sit on the porch and wait for the stars, counting every one until there were too many to count."

"Those days were good." Jamie bends over and pulls up another onion.

"Momma would be very unhappy with the bad stuff going on around here." Gabby clicks her tongue, then turns to leave. "I'm going to go find the men. I'm tired of waiting for Brett. I promised Lady I would take her for a walk and I'm not one to break a promise."

On her way back to the barn, she walks toward the corral. She's on a mission after a failed Plan A. Since Brett didn't come to her, she'll go and find him. Their day was ruined yesterday and she's not about to let that happen today

Hearing a noise, she follows in the direction of a chant that's almost like a repeated lullaby. She pokes her head around the side of the barn and there stands the man whose name refuses to give her rest. Her plan to find Brett is detoured but just for a bit. She's got some unfinished business.

His shirt is brown plaid, and the blue bandana around his neck is wet with sweat. A Stetson on his head. His sleeves are rolled up on his forearms and his boots thick with mud. He's in the corral and, with the mud, he must have cleaned the horse stalls and filled the troughs with fresh water.

"Ma'am," he says as he tips his hat. "Ya daddy's not here. Neither be ya man."

"I didn't come for them. It's you I need to speak with."

"Ya don't say." He wipes his brow.

She slides her backpack from her shoulders, keeping it close. "Seems I had some visitors yesterday and they kept mentioning your name. You wouldn't know anything about that, would you?"

Pablo rubs his chin. "Can't say that I do."

"I think differently. No other man by the name of Pablo works here but you. You want to rethink your answer?"

A staring match ensues and she's not going to be the one to blink or look away.

"Imagine that, little princess...out of her castle, getting her boots all muddy, demandin' answers from me. I work here for years and you never so much as gave me the time of day." He smirks. "Careful there, girly." He spits tobacco juice on the ground in her direction and some of the brown liquid runs down his chin. "And what if I am this Pablo? What can you do?" He walks over to her.

She stands her ground.

He gets in her face. "Just you and me here, sister. How tough are ya?" He reaches up, grabs her chin with his dirty hand and gets in her face.

She knocks his hand away. "You're disgusting."

His temper flares and he pushes her to the ground. "Not so tough, like I thought." He laughs. "How dare you come down here all high and mighty. Ya daddy can't help ya now, stupid beetch."

He gets the burner phone out of his pocket. "Come over, I got her."

Putting the phone down, he finds a Model 25 Smith and Wesson aimed at his chest.

"Aren't you full of surprises. I'm guessin' that yer daddy taught you how to fire that. Shouldn't go pointin' a gun at a person, unless you fixin' on usin' it. Now that we're sharing secrets, wonder how that fence got down. Made sure they weren't findin' those cattle any time soon. You, princess, played right into my hands."

"I know how to use it." Her voice steady but her hands shake from pointing the gun.

Pablo says, "If you're gonna fire that thing, you better do it."

A car pulls into the drive and follows the path to the barn. Detective Harrison jumps out.

"Pablo, I'll take it from here." He looks to Gabby. "Give me the gun."

She shakes her head and bites her lip, aiming her gun alternately between both men.

"Miss King, give me the gun. Pointing a weapon at a detective is serious business."

"Oh, really. How about pointing a gun at a crooked detective? How much is Lopez paying you?" She moves the gun from one man to the other. "You haven't done one thing to speed this investigation along. You've done everything you can to give Lopez time to get away."

"It's over, Gabby. Drop the gun."

She shakes her head again. "Not happening." He reaches to grab the gun from her.

The sound of a pump shotgun echoes. "Not so fast." A voice comes from the side of the barn. Jamie stands with a shotgun pointed at Detective Harrison. "Gabby, you okay?"

Gabby nods.

"Good, now this is what we're gonna do. Gabby, you keep your gun on Pablo and I'll keep mine on our detective. Sheriff Mac's on his way."

"Crazy bitches." Harrison turns toward his car.

Jamie fires her rifle into the air and quickly pumps it. "Next one's not going to miss, Detective. If you're innocent, you have nothing to worry about."

Pablo points a finger at Harrison. "You said they'll never find out. You said—"

"Shut up, you fool."

CHAPTER 40

King Ranch, Northern Pasture

King and Brett are out on horseback by the downed fence, searching for the handful of cattle without success. Rusty joins them coming from the opposite direction.

Rusty says, "Looks like it's three missing. I checked the tags."

Brett scratches his head. "I don't understand. We rode the entire perimeter of this pasture. The fences were fine. We haven't had a storm. I don't get it."

"Maybe a pack of coyotes knocked it over but there's no evidence of that either. Cattle usually wander when food or water is in short supply. That isn't the case. We've checked a farther distance then they would have grazed unless they were spooked or perhaps we've got some rustling going on. Although I didn't find any tire tracks."

King sits straighter. He's very familiar with the sound of a shotgun. "Brett, you hear that?"

"Sure did—what do you think?"

"Sounds like it came from the direction of the house."

"Sounded like that to me, too. With everything that went on yesterday, I'm concerned. Gabby's not in a good place." He glances down at his watch. "I told her I'd be back over an hour ago."

"I hear you. Let's go."

They turn and gallop back to the homestead.

CHAPTER 41

By the time, King and Brett arrive at the barn, Sheriff Mac has Pablo and Detective Harrison in handcuffs. He's waiting for backup as he needs to separate the two men to get them to the station in town. Right now he needs to follow protocol to the letter. Gabby, Rita, and Jamie are huddled together. Brett and King slow their horses' pace and share a glance.

King's the first to remark, "What the hell? Anyone hurt?" He directs this question to the three women. After observing that all are unharmed and there's no evidence of blood, then he addresses his loyal and trusted friend. "Mac, what's going on here?"

"I'm not exactly sure. I need to get statements from everyone. Every 'i' needs to be dotted and every 't' needs to be crossed. The Feds will be all over this. I'm sure these two," he points to the two men on the ground, "will collaborate their stories and basically it could come down to which story the Feds chose to believe—Gabby's and Jamie's account of these here events or their own man, and we all probably know how that's going to go. I'm going to take heat just for bringing

Harrison in, but with your daughter pointing a gun at them and Jamie shootin' a shotgun and making threats..."

King rubs his forehead. "Wow, okay. This is a problem." He turns to his daughter. "Gabby?"

Gabby starts to explain.

"Stop, I can't have anyone saying anything right now. Out of respect, I haven't put your daughter in handcuffs, and if any other officer were here, she'd be cuffed and her rights read to her. King, this is a messy situation. She could be charged with aggravated assault with a deadly weapon. It's best Gabby doesn't say a word until she has an attorney." He shakes his head. "I'm sorry. This is where we're at."

"I've searched Pablo. He has a knife but it's still in the sheath. Pushing Gabby is the only thing I got for a self-defense plea but that is pretty sketchy."

"You're arresting Gabby. She needs to go to the station?" Brett asks.

"That's right." The sheriff takes off his hat and paces. A second patrol car is coming down the drive toward them.

Detective Harrison laughs. "Aggravated assault is jail time. King, your little girl is going to jail. She's crazy. Waving her gun around. She could have killed us." He nods toward Pablo.

"You deserve everything you get." Gabby's harsh tone causes Brett to raise his eyebrows. It's as though he doesn't know this woman.

After Sheriff Mac secures the two men in the police cars, he turns to them. "Gabby and Jamie, you both need to come down to the station. Call your lawyer." He tips his hat. "Don't linger, I'll hate to send an arrest warrant." He looks to King. "I'm being generous; I need to trust that you'll bring them in."

"You got it. We'll be there in short order."

Mac opens his car door.

King calls after him, "Mac, thank you."

CHAPTER 42

The Kings take two cars to the station. Brett and Gabby drive their own vehicle as Brett wishes to stay in town in case the attempted murder charge sticks. The once-defiant Gabby sits staring out of the window. Brett is quiet on the drive. Gabby can read the disappointment in his face, and his actions or lack thereof are cause for more anxiety.

As they near the station, he reaches over the console and squeezes her hand as if to say *I'm here for you.* She bites the inside of her cheek and a tear rolls down her cheek. She turns once more to the window. Having the gun for protection could be misread as premeditated murder. She never thought of that, and as her daddy pointed out back at the ranch, she must not have been thinking at all. Even King could not use his influence to get her out of this one.

Gabby has never been inside a police station. She's watched shows on television. This station has a new location and a new building because, as the city grew, the older historical building no longer could meet the needs to accommodate the additional staff. The older attached jail with its three cells was also inadequate. Unfortunately, as the city's population expanded so did the crime rate.

The building is constructed with the popular Texas white limestone. There are beds of bluebonnets planted around flagpoles that have the U.S. flag, Texas state flag, and the city flag waving in the breeze, making a slight clanging noise when hitting the post. Gabby is glad the sun is shining as she thinks that a positive sign.

Brett parks the car in the police lot, next to King's SUV. They gather together in a huddle. If looks could tell all, Jamie is Jamie; she seems to have an attitude that everything is as normal. She smiles at Gabby and places her arm around her waist as if to give assurance that everything is going to be okay.

King says, "First, we'll wait for Richard. He's assured me that Mr. Mitchell is the best lawyer for this kind of thing and has some clout with the judge. Gabby and Jamie, tell your version of what happened and don't embellish. Answer the questions with facts. Not a word to anyone other than Mitchell. Always look to him before answering. We're paying for his expert advice. Got it?" He lowers his head as if in prayer. "May God be with us."

****

After stating their intentions at the front glassed window with the receptionist, the group is divided. Gabby is read her Miranda rights and led back through a door that must be locked as a buzzer sounded before opening. She looks over her shoulder to Brett, and nods toward Jamie. She hopes that this isn't goodbye.

An officer leads her down a narrow hallway into an interrogation room. The room is empty except for a table, chairs and a mirror, which she guesses is a two-way mirror like the ones on the television shows. Shortly after the door closes, Richard stands in the doorway. He's in a dark gray suit with a tie hanging loose and the shirt's top button open at the collar. His normal collected, calm self, replaced with concern. His actions are fast and he runs his fingers through his dark hair.

"Gabby, I got here as fast as I could. Mr. Mitchell will be here shortly." He hugs her, then pulls back at arm's length and studies her face. "How are you doing? Can I get you anything?"

The sincerity she reads in his eyes is reminiscent of the man she remembers when they had first started dating three years prior. During their time together, he changed to a point where she found it hard to recognize the man she had felt worthy of her love. This profound revelation in these brief seconds causes her to ponder if her relationship with Brett is suffering in the same fashion. With the events of the past few days, is she becoming someone different?

She appreciates the senator's concern for her welfare and is aware that he canceled meetings. "Don't say a word to the cops until you talk to Mitchell," he says. "You're in great hands. I'll do whatever it takes. "

It becomes difficult to maintain their eye contact; she lowers her chin and her shoulders droop.

He pulls her close and she struggles to keep her composure. She feels weak and collapsing in his arms seems easy. *What have I done?*

The door opens and Sheriff Mac, accompanied by a younger officer, a middle-aged man dressed in a dark suit, and a stenographer.

Richard reaches out his hand to the man in the dark suit. "Mr. Mitchell, thank you so much for taking this case, my personal gratitude. This is Gabriella King."

Mitchell reaches out his hand. "Ma'am."

"Let's get started," says Sheriff Mac. He motions for all to sit.

Mitchell says, "Sorry for just getting here, but I need to speak with my client before we begin."

"Of course." The sheriff motions for the others to leave the room. "Ten minutes should be enough."

"Thank you, Sheriff," says Mitchell.

Mitchell pulls up a chair and motions Gabby to do the same. Then he produces a diet Coke, two plastic cups and a small bag of Fritos from his suit pocket. Gabby wonders exactly where it was hiding and ponders what other goodies he has stowed away.

"Please share a drink. You can tell me your story. They can wait." He motions toward the door then pops the top and pours the soda into the glasses. Gabby smiles; she's beginning to like this Mr. Mitchell. Fritos are her favorite; how did he know?

CHAPTER 43

The door buzzes and Gabby, accompanied by Mitchell and Richard, walk through to meet those waiting. Upon seeing his daughter, King hops up from his chair immediately. One by one the others join.

Mitchell addresses them. "Gabby's free to go, charges have all been dropped." There are sighs of relief around the room. "Sometimes we can get aggravated assault reduced to simple assault but we had some unusual circumstances in this case, which I can't get into. We got everyone to agree it was a misunderstanding. Gabby's dropping the assault and battery charges against Pablo.

"Pablo initially demanded a restraining order and for Gabby to have a psychological evaluation. After some persuasion with the help of explaining the charges he was up against, he came to his senses. He's dropping charges against her and we're giving him exoneration in exchange for his full cooperation and information about the Lopez operation. However, this whole ordeal puts a black mark on Detective Harrison and the FBI. Without any formal charges filed and with Pablo's cooperation, it should go away."

"So Pablo is involved?" King's tone is one in disbelief.

"Appears so...Gabby was right about that. She went about it the wrong way, but now she understands that the authorities are handling this and they will greatly appreciate her allowing them to do their job. I made the plea that she's emotionally distraught by the break-in and destruction of her property. However, next time, the Feds won't be so lenient and if she interferes in their investigation a second time, they won't hesitate to lock her up. Assault with a deadly weapon can be up to twenty years in jail and a heavy fine."

He looks to Gabby and Brett. "Ms. King, or should I say Mrs. Matthews, has orders to stay away from the ranch until Lopez is in custody. She's agreed to surrender her firearm. Those are the conditions the FBI recommends and I tend to agree."

King nods his head in understanding. "And for Jamie?"

"She's free to go. Sheriff Mac in his statement said that Jamie stopped the incident from escalating."

King nods again and lets out a huge sigh. "Thank you. I appreciate all you've done."

"One more thing, Ms. King's agreed not to leave town... for any reason."

"Thank you for everything," Gabby says and extends her hand to the attorney.

"You understand?" He continues to hold her hand. "You got lucky this time."

"Yes, I'll behave." She gives him a wink.

Richard nods his head in agreement and shakes King's and Mitchell's hands.

"Thanks, Richard." She holds out her hand to him. He takes it then pulls her close, giving her a hug, and whispers in her ear before turning to leave.

With this good outcome, the group exits the building in better spirits than when they entered a few hours earlier. Immediately, Gabby pulls King away to the side of the parking lot for a father-daughter chat. Following another brief conversation with the family, they part ways.

As mandated, Gabby, along with Brett, will remain in town at their condo. The rest of the party will return to the ranch and carry on with their daily duties. Pablo will return to the ranch and continue to work with Detective Harrison. All are hopeful that with this understanding, Lopez will be in custody soon and his entire operation shut down.

CHAPTER 44

In Town

What were you thinking?" Brett says before starting the car.

"Brett, I don't need a lecture."

"You pulled a gun on Harrison?"

"No, I pulled a gun on Pablo, but only after he admitted he was working for Lopez and pushed me down. First, it was self-defense and, second, I was making a citizen's arrest, then Harrison wanted the gun, I refused."

"Do I have to watch your every move?"

"I was right about Pablo. I knew it." Her voice is strong and she's animated. "I didn't understand why we weren't given protection. I didn't understand Detective Harrison's failure to question Pablo. There was so much I didn't understand. I got angry that nothing was being done."

"So you took it upon yourself. Do you know how crazy that sounds?" He shakes his head again. "It's crazy. I hope you're done. You heard the lawyer. Next time, you'll be in jail."

She rubs his arm. "I'm sorry I caused you worry. I put the gun in my backpack to feel safe. I didn't want another incident like yesterday."

"That's an understatement. None of us want an incident like yesterday. And we certainly don't need another incident like today. And what's up between you and Senator Wright? All of that hugging and what did he say to you? It looks like the two of you are the best of friends. Doesn't the important Senator Wright have other stuff to do than come to the aid of a former girlfriend?"

"He came for Daddy. Daddy funds his campaigns."

"I didn't see him hugging your dad."

"You're jealous," she chides. "Admit it. Just because we had a relationship in the past doesn't mean we can't be friends."

"I don't trust him and I certainly don't like him ...around you."

"He's changed. He's not as hard and driven. I think the job as senator with all of the responsibilities has humbled him." She touches Brett's curl. "I don't have feelings for him—I married you, remember." He gives a smile, heading for the freeway as she reaches over and holds his hand.

"Now, with this time together, we're on a mini-vacation. We can sleep in, go play tennis, see our friends at the club. I'll check for tickets for the opera and the symphony. Daddy has box seats." She rubs his arm. "I can visit all the galleries, talk to some of my artist friends. We can go to a different restaurant every night." She thinks for a few seconds. "I'll need to shop for some clothes. I don't have nearly what I need, as I moved most of my things to our ranch house. This will turn out to be fun."

"Your dad and Rusty, I fear, will have a different opinion. Springtime on a ranch is a busy season. I have work to do. I can't stay here and play when there are things to do on the ranch. Sorry, princess, don't mean to burst your bubble."

"They'll have to manage without you. Because you're all mine. I need a security guard and clearly a chaperone as I tend to misbehave." She smiles.

"Gabby, what am I to do with you?"

"You can give me at least a few days. We deserve that. We hardly spend time together anymore. You're working the ranch. I'm at the horse center. Daddy's fundraiser kept us busy. We need some time for us. Okay?" Her eyes speak sincerity and he's overcome with love.

"I guess it can't hurt. Your dad wants someone to watch you and that someone is me."

"Wonderful. Let's start by going to the club, get a game of doubles going. Since it's such a beautiful warm day, let's have dinner at one of the restaurants on the lake. I do miss all of this at times."

"With you in town, Rita will have you working at the gallery. It won't be all play, princess."

"Don't be a spoilsport."

"Whoever wins in tennis gets to pick out the next activity."

"That's not exactly fair, Brett."

"All's fair in love and war." He winks and his green eyes sparkle. "Tennis it is, then dinner on the lake."

PART IV

CHAPTER 45

Equine Center

It's a busy day for Stan at the center. Every appointment slot is filled due to the rain cancellations from the prior week. This isn't a good time for Gabby to take time off but he's in agreement that after the break-in yesterday, she needs a day to regroup. When he first found Marie, he never imagined the harm this would bring to the people he cared about at the ranch. He picks up his cell to dial Marie but then remembers that she's in protective custody. She won't have her phone. He sure does miss her and wonders if she feels the same about him. A smile lights his face when he recalls their night under the stars. Yes, he's certain that she'll remember his stellar performance.

On his desk is a package the therapist had signed for from the delivery truck. It's addressed to him and not to the center as most of their mail is. Plus, there is no return address, which is also unusual. He shakes the box and something light moves back and forth. Retrieving his knife from its sheath, he slides it through the seam on the box, cutting the plastic tape. Inside the tissue wrap is a card attached to a small envelope. He opens the card first.

> *Dear Stan,*
>
> *I hope you are doing well. I can't thank you enough for everything that you did and all your family is doing in the search for Alexa. I pray that she will be found soon. I am anxious to hug her and to introduce her to my hero!*
>
> *I'm in hiding and safe. Seeing a therapist is not possible until Lopez is caught so I have been doing self-hypnosis and journaling. It is helping. I miss you.*
>
> *The officer was great to mail this package for me. I look forward to the night we can stargaze again and perhaps share a sleeping bag.*
>
> *In the envelope, my gift as promised.*
>
> *All my love, Marie*

Her note erases any doubt...perhaps share a sleeping bag—yep, he's going to count that as conformation that the sex between them was more than an obligatory thank-you; it was real.

Using his knife, he slices the envelope and inside is a steel comb. It is engraved: *Stan, My Indiana Jones, My Hero.* With everything that's transpired, he had forgotten her promise. Now, he closes his eyes and remembers her leaning with her brunette locks hanging over her face as she struggled pulling his plastic comb through her tangles.

Suzanne, the therapist, is standing in his doorway. "You were so deep in thought I didn't want to interrupt. It must have been a happy one, you were smiling." She clears her throat. "I'm finished for the day. You want to go and get a drink or something?"

He leans back in his chair. "Some other time. I've got a lot going on back at the ranch. Raincheck?"

She nods. "See you tomorrow."

CHAPTER 46

King Ranch

Dinner conversation is a buzz after the events of the day. Stan has never seen Jamie so talkative and excited. In between serving the ribeye steaks and the baked potatoes, she's been giving another detail of the drama. Today's events seem to be the highlight of the decade for the older woman whom he looks to as a second mother. He feels like he missed a major action film as he is the only one at the table who was not witness to the Detective Harrison Episode of Gabby's Rage, the pet name given for the events of today.

It's hard for him to envision Gabby pulling a gun on Pablo and then refusing Harrison to the point where Jamie fires a shotgun and the sheriff hauls them all away to the station. This was the stuff of the Wild West. His news about Marie's package is small compared to this drama so he'll keep it to himself.

With Gabby's and Brett's seats empty around the dinner table, he's surprised that he misses them. Maybe he's adjusting to their marriage better these days.

"Stan, how was your day at the center?" asks Rita.

"Busy, but good. The therapist is great. Some of them ask a thousand questions, but Suzanne's helped before so it's good. And she's familiar with the routine and where things are kept. She sings in French when she doesn't think anyone is listening. I like her."

King says, "I'm glad to hear that as Gabby is under strict orders and can't be at the center. Well, more accurately, she has orders to stay away from the ranch. She'll be at her condo until sheriff lifts the restrictions." King rubs his belly. "With everything that has gone on for the past two days, I think it for the best. By the way, Rusty, my man here, brought those cattle back to the pasture. Pablo 'fessed up as to where he took them."

"You're keeping Pablo employed after what went down today?" Stan asks.

"No choice. How's that familiar saying, 'Keep your friends near and your enemies

closer.' The FBI assures me that he'll walk the line. We'd be good to watch Pablo but let's keep an eye on Harrison as well." King turns to Jamie. "Keep your shotgun handy."

"Don't you never mind. I got her right here."

Rusty says, "That's my gal. You done real good today. Proud of ya."

CHAPTER 47

Country Club

Brett and Gabby pick up their racquets at the condo, put the top down on his Audi and drive the short distance to the tennis club. One would never guess that Gabby could have been facing charges of aggravated assault with a deadly weapon earlier this afternoon.

A handful of friends are on the courts and Gabby watches as Brett plays a doubles match with some of his old tennis buddies. She succumbed to their pleas to have Brett complete their foursome, and from his smile and cheerful demeanor, her decision gives her comfort as she feels it makes up for some of the stress she has put him through. She and Brett can play tomorrow when all of these other men will be at their jobs.

Sitting here watching reminds her of their first days together as a couple. With his good looks and dashing mannerisms, he was the focus of many women's conversations. It truly is a miracle that they are husband and wife. It seems the more she resisted, the harder he pursued, and over time he won. Or she would like to believe that she allowed him to win. Now, here on the bleachers, watching him excel in the sport that used to be his life, she ponders why he traded his life on the court for life on the ranch.

Thinking of the ranch prompts her to call Stan. When he doesn't answer, she leaves a message. "Sorry about leaving you alone at the center. Suzanne's great and is the scheduled therapist for the week. I hope to be there in a few days. If you have any questions, call me."

CHAPTER 48

King Ranch

That night in his bedroom, Stan takes out the metal comb and places it on his dresser. It was genuinely thoughtful of Marie and he's anxious to see her again. Not having any contact, without a date for their reunion, is troubling, although he completely understands the need for silence. His greatest wish is for her to be safe after the ordeal she has survived and for Lopez to be behind bars.

He'd breathe easier if he understood how the Feds are managing the case. In the ten days since Marie shared her ordeal, one would think the agency could get the evidence they need for a conviction. He shudders thinking of the latest victims, innocent women just like Marie and Alexa. This sick operation needs to be shut down.

Is Detective Harrison stringing them along as Gabby suggests? Is he one of Lopez' puppets? Or is the blame on the government with its bureaucracy and red tape? These thoughts keep him awake and he has tossed and turned for the past few hours.

In the wee hours of the morning, an unusual noise causes Ryder to stir. Its volume increasing, Stan parts the curtains wide enough to view three helicopters overhead. There's an Air Force base approximately fifty miles away and it's possible they are on a practice drill. However, is it a coincidence that they are flying in the direction of the airstrip?

****

A few hours later, a knock on his bedroom door arouses him.

"Stan, it's rock-and-roll time," King says.

"I don't believe I understand." Stan sits up in bed and checks the time.

King cracks the door and puts his head inside. "Last night, the agency made a run for Lopez. Yesterday, his plane landed on the airstrip and he went to the marijuana farm. They ran a mission, arrested a few, but Lopez got away. Several of the team are after him but with the wide-open landscape they lost him in the dark. They called in reinforcements; you probably heard the choppers. Mac texted me giving me the heads-up, but you didn't hear that from me. The Feds blocked all the roads south, so his only way out is through our ranch. It will take the agency a few hours to get additional men here. But I'm here and I can't stand around and do nothing. I'm not letting that bastard get away."

"What do you need from me?"

"You in?"

"Of course."

"Bring your drone and, Stan, better get your gun. Meet you downstairs."

"Yes, sir."

Ten minutes later, the coffee is brewing. Two large thermoses are on the counter. King is frying eggs in a pan. Stan stands in awe as he has never thought King domestic. At this early morning hour, he seems to know his way around the kitchen.

King waves the spatula in the air. "My calculations from your drone footage say the airstrip is a full eight hours away. Lopez will avoid coming near there as he knows the Feds will be waiting, so he'll take a longer route to the south. The Feds will be there as well, so there's no place to hide." King pauses to scramble the eggs.

"However, if Lopez initially goes south, loses the Feds in the dark, then he might change direction, take to the ridge and travel north. The Feds can cover the southward direction, and I hope Lopez takes that route. But what if—what if Mr. Lopez doubles back a spell, follows the ridge north. Then, he'll end up by our oil wells. There's plenty of roads, some paved, some not, that are used for the oil tankers. If Lopez goes north, he can be a free man." He shakes his head.

"Not on my watch. That's where we come in. We take the Jeep, and your drone, and we go north. I know this land like the back of my hand. I know the paths made by the coyotes and the wild horses along the ridge. I know the dead-ends of the ravines. I know the rivers and lakes. There aren't that many ways to get north. When the Feds come up empty and they finally figure out that he went north, Lopez will be long gone."

Stan scratches his head. "Wow, that's some plan."

"It's a good plan. If I were Lopez, it would be my plan." He dishes the eggs out on the plates. "If I'm wrong, you and I got ourselves a nice day—traveling around, enjoying the sunshine, checking out the perimeters of the ranch. Maybe we should take fishing poles." He chuckles.

"I find no harm in going but much harm if we don't. Lopez needs to be behind bars for what he has done to Marie. But what if Lopez comes straight for the ranch? Who will be here to protect my mother and Jamie?"

"I'll leave Rusty and, from yesterday, Jamie proves that she can handle herself with a shotgun. Your mother never wanted much to do with a pistol. Maybe after all of this is over, she may come around. In the past year, she's refused every time I offered to teach her."

King motions for Stan to sit at the table and places a loaf of bread in front of him.

"Eat up, son. A man can't do a good job when he's thinking more about his stomach then the work at hand."

"Good idea. Besides, the batteries for the drone need to charge."

"It's gonna be a good day, son." King raises his coffee cup.

CHAPTER 49

Downtown

Gabby and Brett are lying in bed, her head resting on his chest, and he runs his fingers through her blond strands.

"The delivery guy will be here. I need to get up. Move over, princess."

"I'll move over but I'm not getting up." She slides over and enjoys the warmth of the soft sheets against her naked body.

He kisses her on the forehead. "You don't have to. Stay here. I will bring you breakfast in bed."

"You're so sweet to order us breakfast."

"I'm sure you can find a way to repay." He winks.

As he dons his sweatpants, the doorbell rings. "Be back in a jiffy." He grabs his wallet as he passes the dresser. She still marvels at his physique. Working on the ranch as well as training for the rodeo has defined his entire body. She smiles, thinking his low-riding sweats accentuate his lean waist and hips. His rancher's tan is a bit weird. She'll suggest that they take her daddy's boat and spend the day on the lake. Nearly a year has passed since she's done that. It will be good for her soul and could offer a fix for Brett's odd-looking tan lines.

He comes back to the bedroom with a tray. "This is just the coffee and the sticky buns." The aroma of the coffee entices her to yawn and stretch with her arms up in the air.

"Coffee smells great. Brett, we could take this time for the honeymoon we never had. With our decision for a quick wedding and then traveling to Vegas for the National Rodeo Championships, we didn't take any time for us."

"I'd like that. I got a text from your dad. He says to take all the time we need. His exact words," Brett reads from his phone, "'Don't concern yourself with the ranch, my daughter needs you more.'"

"Daddy's always looking out for me."

"I believe your actions yesterday caused alarm. Do you get for one second just how lucky you are to be here with me and not in jail?"

"Please, no lectures. Don't spoil our day. I admit, I was out of line."

"I need to hear that, Gabby. What you did yesterday does not fit into what one would describe as normal behavior."

"Lots of things aren't normal. Having one's house broken into is not normal. Having men threaten to kidnap me is not normal. Then there's Marie—she was held hostage, escaped and almost died. That isn't normal, Brett."

"Hey, hey, I understand. When you were at the police station yesterday, your daddy and Sheriff Mac had a conversation. These men have known you all your life and have your best interest at heart, and all of us are sorry for not understanding. The point I'm making is that to get you released, your daddy promised Mac that you would see your therapist. You have an appointment later this morning. King messaged that as well."

"Wow, really, you all think I'm unstable."

He takes her hands in his. "No, that's not it at all. You just listed all of the abnormal stuff. See the therapist so your obligation is complete and when she reports that you're fine, it will be over. Hey, look at me." He lifts her face to be level with his. "This is easy. I'll be there waiting and then we can play the rest of the day. As you said, this is our honeymoon. I certainly don't want to spend my life looking at you across a table on visitation day." He smiles.

"If I have to." She bites her upper lip.

"That's my girl. I'll heat up our omelets."

"Thanks. I love you."

"Love you too, princess."

CHAPTER 50

The Great Lake

A few hours later after Gabby's appointment with the therapist, Brett's behind the wheel of the twenty-three-foot Cobalt, cruising away from the marina. The white puffy clouds reflect in the still water. "Which way, princess, toward the dam or away from it?"

"Let's go toward the dam. There's more restaurant choices for lunch." She smiles admiring his muscular frame, with sunglasses that make him look like Matthew McConaughey.

"You got it." He turns to the right following the shoreline. A blue heron takes flight in front of them and several turtles that were sunbathing on the rocks slide gracefully into the water.

"The sun feels wonderful. I didn't realize how much I missed this lake. Coming here on a weekday is heaven. We practically have the whole lake to ourselves. Awesome. We need to do more of this." He looks forward, and stands at the wheel, the wind blowing his hair.

"Brett, let's find a cove and just float for a bit. I want to work on my tan. It's nonexistent but that will be fixed after today." She sits in the V of the front of the boat facing him and removes her bikini top. She throws it at him, laughing. "It's legal to go topless in Texas. Besides, tan lines won't look good with my dress." She raises her arms and puts her hair back in a ponytail. Brett's eyes never leave her and she returns his smile. It's as though they left all of their cares and worries behind.

"Yes, ma'am." He winks. "You aren't going to get an argument from me." He turns up the pop music on the radio and sings along. Even his dimple seems to smile.

She turns her wedding band around on her finger. These past five months as Mrs. Matthews have been great. However, the events of the past weeks are disturbing, causing her to reflect. She recalls her daddy's words that opening the Equine Assisted Therapy Center would be a full-time job and as usual he was right. She's there every day and barely has the time for anything else. Now that the center is established, maybe she should hire another employee. She makes a mental note to bring that up with Stan the next time they talk. Several other discussions need to happen. Stan's future intentions are at the top of that list. Since there's nothing she can decide about any of that now, it'll be best to enjoy this spectacular day.

Spending quality time with Brett has been magical. They've played tennis with old friends and even though they have a court at their house on the ranch, it's not the same as having friends join in a doubles game. Today, they're out on the lake, something they used to do on a weekly basis, and tonight they'll dine at an upscale Italian restaurant followed by the symphony. She'll wear her new strapless minidress, the reason to discard the swimsuit top.

On this trip, they've yet to visit ArtSmart, and she's surprised that Rita hasn't mentioned her working a shift or two. Perhaps Rita shares the view of her daddy and Brett, that her behavior with the gun was foolish and she needs time off. She loves living at the ranch but the other half of her enjoys this life. There has to be a way to mesh the two. Why can't she have it all?

She observes Brett at the helm, and wonders what he's thinking at this moment. Does he share her same thoughts? She leans her head against the seat back. Life is good, enjoy it. There's plenty of time to figure all of this out.

Brett steers the boat into a cove and cuts the engine. She lowers the anchor and secures the rope to the cleat. Brett hands her a glass of wine and he has a beer.

"A toast, to us. Our honeymoon." He clicks her plastic cup with his bottle. "Turn around. You're going to get burned." He squeezes suntan lotion into his hand and rubs his hands together. He starts with her shoulders and back, but then his hands circle around and he massages her upper body and neck and works his magic down to her breasts.

"You're getting side-tracked." She moans.

He kisses her neck. "I'm just following your lead." His hand slips inside her bathing suit bottom. "What were you saying about tan lines?" He laughs.

Their bodies greasy from shared suntan lotion glisten in the warm sun. Gabby closes her eyes. Hours of therapy in the psychologist office can't compare to this therapy, this experience...naked, making love under the sun with the gentle rhythm of rolling waves. She wishes to stay in this place, forgetting her concerns and worries.

He rolls on top and kisses her so gently that she reaches her hands around his neck and pulls him toward her.

"Princess, can't do that."

"Why not?"

"A boat's coming." He hands her a towel and pulls on his swim trunks.

"Hello, officers." Brett waves to the Lake Patrol as they approach.

"Everything all right?"

"Everything is great. Just enjoying this beautiful day."

"We didn't see anyone. Thought you might have engine problems and abandoned."

"No, everything is great."

"Be safe," the driver says with a smile.

"Yes, sir." Gabby and Brett wave goodbye.

Gabby holds back laughing out loud until the boat leaves. "Wow, that was a close call."

Brett's eyes sparkle. "Now, where were we?" He pulls her in tight. "I remember."

CHAPTER 51

King Ranch

The sun has broken the horizon by the time that all supplies are loaded in the Jeep. King explains his plan to Rita. She's not keen on sending her husband and son out to a remote place in search of dangerous men. Stan sees her wringing her hands as they pull away. King is careful to ease on the gas and leave as quietly as possible so as not to alert the ranch hands that anything out of the ordinary is going on.

Driving down the path, Stan checks his Heckler & Koch Mark 23 in the holster before settling back in his seat. He's not used to wearing it but feels the need to keep it close. He holds on to the safety bar and then scans the sky, grateful for a clear day. A few clouds reflect shades of orange and pink; he hopes the warmth it displays is a good omen.

King's plan seems solid. The first few hours of the trip will be easy but after they get to the old windmill, they'll need to focus, paying close attention to their surroundings. If Lopez picks this route for his escape, they should be ahead of him by almost two hours. However, that's not certain so King wants to drive the first four hours at a fast pace. All Stan can do is hold on tight and try to keep his anxiety under control.

King's plans are pretty sophisticated for being thrown together with such short notice. It's close to noon when they pass the windmill and turn in a northeasterly direction to find the gravel path that parallels the ridge. King makes a call to the Feds and they report that Lopez is still missing. Their search is wide and with the limited manpower, it is slow.

As a precaution in case their efforts fail to stop Lopez, and believing that he will fight, rather than surrender, in the event that Lopez slips by, King calls his hired hands for reinforcement. Usually these men guard his oil rigs, which are mostly in the northern territory. They'll scan the landscape, report anything unusual, and they'll even make a citizen's arrest for any trespassers. King has done all in his power to get Lopez into the hands of the authorities.

With the knowledge that the Feds do not have Lopez, upon arrival at the ridge, King and Stan continue to execute their plan. First, they pick an optimal place for King to place the explosives, and for Stan to launch his drone. With the drone's ten-mile radius, after sighting Lopez, they gauge that they'll have approximately a fifteen- to twenty-minute window before showtime.

They're prepared to be outnumbered. Worse odds have been against King in the past, but that never stopped him. However, Stan has never been in any situation that can compare. He's so out of his league, he'll follow instructions and pray for a good outcome.

After picking a level spot, each has his assigned tasks. King mixes the catalyst with the Tannerite compound in quart-sized containers. He'll place these in strategic areas on the west side. His goal is to force Lopez to select a route eastward that will guide him into a dead-end canyon where he'll have to continue on foot. Additionally, the noise and the smoke from the combustion will alert the authorities of their location.

It's Stan's job to climb the ridge for a clear view to launch the quadcopter and scan the footage for possible paths that a vehicle arriving from the south will most likely travel. If Lopez does come, the dust from his vehicle will easily be visible. He works fast and he's grateful that there's a stronger satellite signal on the ridge, as they have driven through areas without that.

He returns to the Jeep with his initial footage, rubs his leg and swallows a pain pill with the last of the coffee from his thermos.

King throws him a camouflage shirt. "Here, you should put this on. You're like a shining beacon up there."

He looks down at his white t-shirt and rubs his chin, taking the shirt. "Sure, didn't think of that."

"Get in." King motions for him to get in the vehicle. "You're now the HVI."

"What's that?"

"Special ops guy—you're a high-value individual. With your skills, when the time is right, your mission is to shoot these here targets. Pay attention.

"I'll show you where I placed them so you can pick the best stakeout place. Some place out of sight." King then raises his left forefinger in the air. "This here is the sign. Got it?"

Stan nods his head.

"When I put my finger in the air, count to three, then fire. As long as my finger is up, you keep counting to three and firing, one target after another. If my finger goes down, stop."

"What is this stuff?"

"Tannerite, binary rifle targets."

"You need a license for that?"

"Only when it's mixed. These are extenuating circumstances. Stick with me, boy, and this old cowboy will show you a few things."

"Can these hurt someone?"

"Sure, if they get too close. Men have lost arms and legs playing with this stuff. They make quite a boom, hear it seven miles away. Just gonna scare 'em, that's all. If they turn around, the Feds can pick 'em up. If they go into the ravine, they hit a dead-end. It's much like herding cattle."

Eight different targets are set in strategic places all within a hundred feet. Stan picks a central firing place under a few bushes to the right of where King will block the path with the Jeep. He puts on his goggles, checks the scope, and aims to ensure that all of the targets can be seen. Now would be the time for adjustments. He would love a few practice shots but that would alert Lopez.

Stan checks his watch. "Getting closer. I should launch the quad-copter again."

This time King follows him to the top of the ridge. Stan limps a bit but the pain medicine seems to have eased it some.

"See anything?" King stands with his hands on his hips.

"Not yet. What do we do now?"

"Just wait. Have a sandwich. We missed lunch."

"Eat, now?" He raises his eyebrows observing the calm demeanor of the older man.

"Sure, like I said this morning, a man can't do a good job when he's thinking more about his stomach than the work at hand." King smiles, pats him on the back and hands him a sandwich from his backpack.

Stan takes a bite and chews. His stomach is doing flip-flops but King acts as though it's business as usual.

"Stan, I want to thank you for all that you've been doing. I see your efforts—learning to ride, herding cattle, and helping Gabby at the center. I see you struggle with the leg and with your heart. Especially with matters of the heart, makes no sense at all why one person falls for one or another. Gabby's happy so that makes me happy. Your mother worries about you, more than she lets on. She wants you to be happy." He looks away and finishes his sandwich.

"You're in a position where you can do whatever you want. Guess you've found out that money doesn't equate with happiness." King stares at him. "Don't worry, I haven't said a word to Rita. It's none of my business. The only reason I know is because I have to be careful. Always somebody out there trying to take what doesn't belong to 'em."

He pauses. "I love the land. I love Texas. Today, it means a lot, you here with me. I just wanted to say that...I needed to tell you that. Your mother, you, and Will are my family. I told you that the night before I put a ring on your mother's finger and I meant every word of it. You're family and I'm proud of you."

251

King stands, pats him on the back again. "Better launch that drone again. If Lopez is coming this way, he'll be here soon."

"Yes, sir." Stan places his hands on the control box with a little more confidence.

****

Stan pushes the return-home button on the drone's base. "They're coming up the path next to the cliff, just like you predicted. I saw two four-by-fours. Can't be sure, possibly six men."

King uses his binoculars. "That means it's showtime. Let's get in position. Do whatever it takes to make them steer to the right."

Waiting for the drone to return, Stan checks the sky. Surely the Feds' helicopters are tracking Lopez, although he doesn't hear or see anything. Perhaps the biggest cause for his anxiety is the reality that they are on their own. Where is Detective Harrison? Maybe Gabby was right for not trusting him.

Both men head for the Jeep. Stan's heart is racing and he reminds himself to breathe. Once there, he stows the drone, then with shaky hands grabs the rifle. Still with his pistol around his waist, he takes his station. Waiting, he flexes his fingers trying to loosen them, puts in his ear plugs and dons his goggles, then practices his aim. Looking through the scope he points the rifle at all eight targets, one by one, memorizing their locations. He wipes the sweat from his brow and says a prayer. He doesn't want to let King down.

King also has his Remington 700 rifle and holds a stance in front of the Jeep. He's going to stand his ground, locked and loaded. While he waits, he goes through a mental checklist. He reaches for his cell and leaves a message for Rita, just in case. Earlier this morning, he gave the GPS coordinates to the authorities, another check. *It's a good plan*, he repeats in his head to force doubt away. He rolls back his shoulders and takes in a deep breath.

No turning back now; this is showtime. The engine sounds are getting closer. When they are one hundred feet in front of him, King fires his rifle giving a warning. "You're trespassing," he yells. "Get off my land."

Lopez gets out of the vehicle. "Look at you standing there, giving me orders. You and what army?" Lopez looks around. "Out here all by yourself. Even for you, that is foolish. I won't think twice about putting a bullet through your head." He laughs. "Out of my way, King. Out of respect, I'll pretend that this little meeting never happened."

"I'm not moving."

"Hope you plan on using that rifle because that's what it's going to take."

King puts his arm up halfway as if motioning for Lopez to stop. "You best be headed back where you came from." King sees that two men in the second vehicle are pointing semi-automatic rifles at him.

"Sorry, not an option." Lopez gets back in the vehicle. "Call his bluff. Go around him."

The vehicles move forward, approaching King at a fast pace. He raises his arm above his head. After three seconds, as Lopez is nearly even with King, the first target explodes. King ducks using the Jeep as cover. The ground shakes and a cloud of dust makes visibility impossible.

"What the f—?" Lopez yells.

King speaks in a loud voice, "You said it was foolish for me to come alone. I'm not a fool. Got my men all over." He waves to the land behind him on the left. Then he raises his hand above his head and this time points his finger. Lopez's man has his gun aimed at King and fires. King ducks and hopes that Stan sees that this has become a matter of life and death.

Stan fires not one but three targets. One of the targets blasts as Lopez's truck nears. The noise is deafening; dust and debris fall onto them. The driver spins the vehicle around sharply so that a wheel lifts off the ground. King keeps his arm raised as he rounds the Jeep for protection. Stan fires at the remaining targets. King's glad that Stan is aware of the dire circumstances that they face. Lopez and his men steer off right toward the ravine. As they pass, King raises his rifle at the second vehicle and hits the metal frame. The second Jeep speeds away following Lopez. One of the men turns and fires, so King fires another shot.

Meanwhile, Stan crawls from his position and stands with his pistol pointed in the direction Lopez and his men went. "We're following them, right?"

"You bet, let's herd 'em into the ravine." He's already behind the wheel.

Stan barely jumps into the moving Jeep as King floors the gas pedal. A noise overhead gets their attention. The authorities in the helicopter must have seen the explosions and are on Lopez's trail.

"Perfect timing. Where were they a few minutes ago?" He looks to Stan. "You did good, real good. Let's go have some fun."

He drives to the ravine just behind the Feds' helicopter and blocks the entrance. Lopez is trapped. Stan and King take shelter behind a boulder with their guns ready.

The loudspeaker on the helicopter announces for Lopez to surrender.

King winks at Stan. "We'll let the Feds handle it from here. Glad they finally showed up. Didn't know if we could pull it off, but we did. Your mother would have had my hide if anything would have happened to you." He pats Stan on the back.

"Or mine if something would have happened to you. You had doubts? I thought you were all confident."

"It was fifty-fifty."

"Fifty-fifty, you tell me that now."

"Son, I sure as hell wasn't gonna tell you earlier. You almost pissed your pants as it was." King unbuttons his shirt, revealing a black vest underneath.

"Is that what I think it is?"

"Depends—if you're thinking it's a bullet-proof vest, then the answer is yes."

"OMG."

"Like I said, odds were fifty-fifty." He pats Stan on the shoulder and guides him toward the Jeep.

Both laugh out loud.

CHAPTER 52

The helicopter lands in a clearing a few hundred feet away and Special Agent Rawlings jogs over. He extends his hand, then smiles. "It's a pleasure. Thanks for your help. The boys will be coming through in a few."

He points to the Jeep. "You'll need to move that. The boys are being careful so that everything's done by the book. Don't want Lopez's fancy lawyers getting him off on some bogus legal matter." His hands are on his hips. "In a few minutes, I'll need you to give your statement.

"Lopez must have laid low, then traveled using night vision goggles. This new technology, in the hands of the wrong people, makes our job harder. I still haven't figured out how he avoided the heat sensors. We'll get to the bottom of it though."

He turns and spits. "We had our men searching southward." Rawlings scratches his chin. "Great idea to use the explosives. Our guys were a good twelve miles away. The copter further than that. Detective Harrison gave us these coordinates but we thought he was blowing smoke."

"Where is Detective Harrison?" Stan asks.

"He's making the arrests." Rawlings nods toward the ravine. "He's been working this for a while, went undercover a few months ago. When you picked up Marie, having a witness forced us to move faster than anticipated. A few months ago, Lopez wanted ears on the ranch, to keep you," he points to King, "under wraps. Harrison, now working undercover, finds Pablo at the bar. When your daughter pulled a gun on Pablo, Harrison's cover could have been compromised, all his work for naught. But then, hallelujah, Miss Jamie saves the day. When she aimed that shotgun on Harrison, priceless. Wish I could have seen that. Pablo's back where we needed him. If Harrison was going down, Pablo knew he would go down with him. Pablo starts singing."

The sound of motors approaching shortens the special agent's story. King goes to move the Jeep so they can pass.

Lopez, in cuffs, yells to King, "You're a dead man. Hear me. Both of you."

CHAPTER 53

King Ranch

L ater that night after the excitement from the day's events were retold over dinner, Stan's in his bedroom sitting at the window. He recalls the events as though he's lived a day in the life of a character in an action novel. He sends up thoughts of gratefulness into the star-filled night sky. He knows deep in his soul that the outcome could have had a much different ending. But he's here and he's desperate to share his thoughts about fear and dying, that play in his mind, refusing to be still. He wants to share these thoughts with Marie, but that's not possible.

He picks up the silver comb and reads the inscription again. Today, he's surprised himself because he believes he was as tough as Indiana Jones. He missed one target in the second set of three and had to reshoot but at that point, there was so much chaos going on that it really didn't matter. He settled his nerves and aimed successfully. His silent prayer of thankfulness goes up into the night and he reaches to touch his star tattoo.

After today's events, he's even more worried about Marie than he was before. Instead of improving her situation, now with Lopez in custody, she's in more danger as their star witness since the bulk of the prosecutor's case balances on her testimony. The Feds are taking Lopez's threats seriously and extra security measures have been implemented, with two guards placed at her place of stay, wherever that is.

Also, additional agents have been placed at strategic locations on the ranch. He agrees with King and Sheriff Mac that it was a good idea to get Gabby away from the ranch. King took it on himself to hire guards to watch Gabby's downtown condo. Stan's not sure that Gabby and Brett are aware of the measures taken, as it's probably best that they aren't.

He wonders when it will be safe, and when life will return to normal. He never could have guessed that his search for an airstrip on a yellowed map would bring this much drama and craziness to his family.

CHAPTER 54

In the City

Five days into their impromptu honeymoon, one of Rita's employees at ArtSmart calls out sick. Gabby honors Rita's request to manage the gallery. It's all good as she and Brett have executed most of the plans for their stay in town. In addition to boating, playing tennis, and inviting friends to dinners, they attended the symphony—it wasn't her treasured Beethoven but the fifth symphony "Jupiter Finale," by Mozart—and they also attended the ballet "Coppelia," a popular ballet seen first in 1870 in Paris.

In addition to these cultural outings, Brett has accompanied her on several successful shopping trips as she fell immediately in love with the spring colors of bright blues in the trendy styles showcased in the store windows.

Just yesterday, Brett had rolled his eyes once or perhaps twice during a stroll down Main Street that turned into a shopping spree. She knew she was testing his limits but he didn't tell her no. It was their honeymoon. In one store, she'd found something for him.

"Brett, try this on." She held the light blue and tan plaid sports jacket up to the light.

He took the jacket from her and carefully put his arms through the sleeves, then gave the lapel a tug. Next, he waltzed over to the mirror posing as if he were on a fashion runway.

"What do you think? I look pretty dapper. I can't imagine anyone sporting it better. It's as if it were made just for 'moi.' He pretended to flip his hair back off the collar, followed by a wave of his wrist.

She giggled. "I could insist that we buy it, but..." She thumbs through the rack again and pulled out a navy jacket. "Here, try this one."

"No," he said. "I like this one."

"You're kidding, right?"

Refusing to take it off, even though for a proper fit the sleeves should have been altered, he wore it out of the store.

Once outside, she said, "You're crazy. I need to tell you that. What are you thinking?"

"I can't let you have all the fun. Maybe I shall wear this jacket with my pink shirt. The ladies won't be able to keep their hands off me."

"I don't think so." She shook her head and laughed.

"I have a confession." His look was serious. "I hate plaids."

"You don't say." She bent over laughing hard.

He pointed his finger into the air as if making a proclamation. "However, from this day forward, I vow to wear this plaid jacket on every wedding anniversary until it's threadbare."

Sharing in her merriment, he chuckled so hard he could barely get the words out. They laughed so much that people passing on the street must have thought them insane.

Arriving back at the condo, her closets, already overflowing, lacked space to accommodate her new purchases. Hence, Gabby spent the next few hours pondering which of her clothing would be packed into the now-empty shopping bags recycled to hold discards for Goodwill. This purge instilled a feeling of accomplishment and organization, and she hopes it will assist in taming her rage at the inefficiency of Detective Harrison with the investigation.

The first few days of their honeymoon in town, Brett seemed happy but as the days go on, she senses his restlessness though he never complains. Quite frankly, if he said, "Let's go home," she would agree. Concerned about abandoning the EAT Program, she calls daily but Stan routinely gives a thumbs-up, reporting that all's well and that Suzanne is doing a great job. But still, she worries. She hasn't heard from Sheriff Mac and wonders whether the restriction for her to stay away from the ranch has been rescinded, since she passed the evaluation at her shrink's office. Legally, can she go home?

Earlier after Rita asked her to work, Brett immediately contacted a tennis friend to arrange a game of singles. She's happy that he's out and exercising since there's nothing he can do at the gallery. It will probably be good for their relationship to take a break from one another.

Surrounded by paintings, Gabby stands wide-eyed and carefully studies each piece; as her eyes rest on Nicholas Templeton's work, a burst of inspiration and creativity overcomes her. His bold strokes and use of color offer a challenge as if they are aware that she hasn't painted anything meaningful in a month.

Usually around the lunch hour, client traffic slows so she can paint, and if she's brave enough to move her easel to the showroom, she could paint the entire afternoon. Customers watch in a mesmerized state when an artist works. She thinks it's due to the intoxicating paint smell in combination with the creative ambiance of the surrounding artistic works. All of these things speak to the viewer as if he contributes in the mystery of the final outcome. In many cases the painting sells before the last brush mark graces the canvas.

Inspired by Templeton's daring brush strokes, she finds her paintings lacking and is inclined to incorporate similar strokes on her canvas. Glancing to her wall in the gallery where she replaced the paintings that Lopez purchased the night of the party, she recalls their conversation. Bringing to mind Lopez's touch renders goosebumps to appear on her arms. She shudders, thinking that two of her paintings are in the hands of an evil man.

Her easel, disassembled and buried under a box in the storeroom, confirms that she's abandoned her craft. Later, accessing her paints, she finds some of the tubes hard, and after squeezing them, the tubes split revealing only more dried paint inside. Gabby bites the inside of her cheek, reminded of her daddy's words, "You realize that the horse center will be a lot of work." A smile crosses her face as she thinks of his wisdom and his character. He's a wonderful man, with high ethics and true to his word, representing the opposite of Mr. Lopez.

The ring of the cash register confirms the first sale of the day just shy of the noon hour. The customer is a friend and purchases Rita's twelve-by-twelve still life watercolor of a bunch of onions. Their golden skins appear translucent against a lavender shadow. She makes a mental note to compliment Rita on her technique as she texts a snapshot of the smiling customer with her purchase.

The following hour proves quiet so Gabby increases the volume of the Beethoven symphony on the overhead speakers and gathers the remainder of her painting supplies. With satisfaction, she squeezes paint onto her palette in neat heaps along the exterior. She mixes a pile of a small amount of red with a larger portion of yellow in the middle as her tube of orange was one of the unfortunate tubes that had hardened and subsequently got tossed into the garbage.

Picking up her favorite brush, a one-inch flat, she twirls it into the orange paint and approaches the prepared gessoed canvas. However, after briefly touching the hog's hair to the canvas she steps away, discarding the brush, and searches diligently through her supply bag for a different tool. A minute later, she stares at the large metal gizmo in wonder. It's her biggest palette knife. She has watched demonstrations where artists have painted entire compositions abandoning the popular brush for a palette knife. Can she be so bold?

It seems that Nicholas Templeton at one time took this very step. She swoops the palette knife into the orange heap, lifting the bulk of the paint to the blade. With one quick stroke, she applies it to the canvas. In an effort to clean the palette knife of the remaining paint, she turns the knife on edge, creating a partner for the first. This technique is straightforward and surprising fun. But can she fashion a desirable composition using it? Gathering the cadmium yellow from the palette, she reenacts the same movements. The strokes are vertical in appearance similar to notes on a musical scale bundled tightly. The more she thinks of Detective Harrison, Pablo, the men breaking into her house, the more aggressive her strokes become. Overhead, Beethoven's symphony pairs to perfection as it equals in rhythm as well as emotion. *Dun, dun, dun, dunnn...*

It's difficult for her to keep this fast tempo. Stroke after stroke she lays varying tones of different colors and hues next to each other; some contrast and others enhance. Her energy is high as she works the canvas from top to bottom; stanza after stanza emerges on the composition. Her palette of paints empties quickly. To keep in tempo, she reverts to squeezing the paint from the tubes directly. The method is physically and mentally liberating as one brilliant color after another is showcased. Finally, in contrast to the busy composition, a simple field of yellow ochre fills the open space above the first stanza, giving a title to the musical masterpiece below.

A few hours later, as she is bent over in exhaustion and clearly out of paint, the last of the white canvas is no more. It's been replaced with this high-energy opus in vertical lines of brilliant color. It's as if Beethoven's symphony has been put on canvas.

Standing back and eying her work from afar, she's aware that during the exercise of painting, the canvas converted her rage into energy giving vivacity to the painting. *Voila!* The result is a dramatic symphony for the eyes. She bows in front of the canvas, giving respect similar to a conductor giving tribute to his orchestra following a performance.

With palette knife in hand, she studies her afternoon's work as though in disbelief that she's the creator of this incredible masterpiece.

The bells on the door ring, and Brett slips into the gallery, locking the door behind him. He's done this on several occasions, mostly before closing time. A glance at her watch shows she should have closed fifteen minutes ago.

"Hey there," she says to her beloved. "How was tennis?"

"Great. It's nice to spend time catching up on the latest club gossip. Seems it's been a Peyton Place these past few months. You ready for dinner?"

She looks down at her apron and the paint smears all over her exposed arms and hands. "Not quite. I lost track of time. Give me a few minutes."

He kisses her.

"You smell nice."

"After tennis, I showered and used that new cologne. I'm wearing my new duds. You like them?" He turns a full circle in front of her.

"You look great, as always."

"My wife buys my clothes." He winks, then walks to the easel. "You painted this?"

She nods. "What do you think?"

"It's different." He stands to one side and cocks his neck in the opposite direction as if studying the painting's every detail.

"Different how...like different good or different bad? You need to give me more than different." Her hands are on her hips.

"Not sure yet. I got to get used to it." He rubs his chin. "It's interesting. You've never painted like this before."

"Good for you to notice. That was the point, to paint something bold, more daring."

"You certainly got that." He walks close so that his nose is only a few inches from the canvas.

"It's definitely still wet so be careful. I don't want you to get paint on your new clothes."

Gabby's attention goes to her ringing phone and she answers it before turning back to Brett. "That was Rita checking on us to make sure that we kept the gallery open until closing. I wonder why she would think to say that?" She raises her eyebrows at Brett.

He smiles thinking about their past afternoons when he would lock the gallery door, flip the open sign to closed, giving them time alone in this creative space. "Can't imagine. Hey, I'm the perfect gentleman, never to breathe a word, let alone kiss and tell." He looks back and forth from her to the painting mess.

"I'll clean it up. I really don't want your new clothes ruined. Go get yourself a beer." She makes a motion toward the back room. "I'll hurry, promise."

"No need, we don't have anywhere pressing to go." He returns, twists off the bottle cap and takes a gulp of the beer, continuing to study her afternoon artwork. It is interesting. He's not an art critic but he knows his wife.

"You ready?" She emerges from the backroom in a one-piece pantsuit that shows off her hourglass figure.

"Gab, what's your interpretation?" He points the neck of the beer bottle at the easel.

"You first."

"I see the painting's vertical lines as making a decisive statement. Even though they are all different colors, they're unified, requiring the viewer to agree or simply walk away."

"Wow, that's deep but correct in the sense that the lines are unified. This canvas is my interpretation of Beethoven's Fifth Symphony."

"*Dun, dun, dun, dunnnn...*" He hums.

"Impressive. This art stuff must be rubbing off."

"I know a thing or two. That's how I,"—he hums—"I got you, babe."

She pulls on his arm, motioning toward the door. "Let's go, my Sonny Bono! I'm starved."

CHAPTER 55

Equine Center

The spring air has turned into a warm summer breeze. Gone are the bluebonnets and the Mexican blankets, replaced by black-eyed Susans, daisies, and flowering prickly pear cactus. The horse center is having its most successful month since opening. Suzanne has become a familiar and valuable member of the team. Stan's had drinks with her after work several times. He thinks she would like more from their relationship but he's still holding out for Marie, which is silly and almost as ridiculous as a schoolboy crush on his third-grade teacher. In frustration, he presses too hard with his pencil and the point breaks. *Damn.*

The Lopez trial isn't for another few months. Several times, since Marie was taken into protective custody, he's sent letters through the proper authorities, but only once has he held a letter written by her in return. It seemed that her motivation for this one letter was also to express gratitude. Soon after Lopez's arrest, in a DEA raid, tipped off by one of Lopez's man, her friend Alexa was found in a house of prostitution in Atlanta, nearly dead from a heroin overdose. According to Detective Harrison, she is currently undergoing treatment in a government-run center isolated from the outside world. Grateful, like Marie, that her friend is found and alive, he surmises after deciphering Marie's psychological jargon that she's experiencing survivor's guilt, setting her back a few paces in her own emotional recovery.

The long-waited letter written in a factual tone laced with gratitude, lacked any words of pining or wishing them to be together, so instead of the joy he anticipated, the letter brings disappointment.

The entire situation is complex but at the same time almost non-existent; it is as if he needs an extraordinary alignment of the stars for his wish to come true. He caresses the star on his left shoulder, knowing its loyalty has changed and now shines for this hurting dark-haired woman.

Their relationship was brief and ran high on emotions that in hindsight would cause anyone to question. He recalls her description of their lovemaking as an act of feeling alive and one of thankfulness. He had thought her theory would prove correct for him as well and, given time, his feelings would falter. But as sure as looking up to the heavens on a cloudless night to discover familiar constellations overhead, his love for Marie remains.

He's done his research, knowing what it would take to be with her these next few months. Even if the Feds would allow it, selfish as it may seem and most likely premature without confirmation of her feelings, he's not ready to give up this ranch life that initially was forced on him from his motorcycle accident. He'd like to test their relationship but not at the cost of leaving the ranch. He lets out a deep breath and shakes his head because right now he needs to focus on work. Only a couple of hours are left in the workday and he has yet to complete the accounting. He grabs another pencil from the container on his desk and examines the sharpened lead.

Head down and deep into the numbers in the columns in the accounting books, the slam of a car door gets his attention. Purposeful, fast footsteps are followed by an excited Gabby throwing a newspaper on his desk. Her face is flushed.

"Here, read this, unbelievable! Can't say I have any sympathy." She brushes back her hair.

Stan unfolds the paper and noticing the large print on the first page, he begins to understand.

Lopez Found Dead

"My God," he mutters under his breath as he continues to read past the headline. The words jump off the page. "What—"

"Stan, it's over. Lopez is dead. I don't care if he committed suicide or if someone got to him. It doesn't matter. He's dead."

He leans back in the chair, his mind racing trying to remember from his days as a lawyer all of the ramifications of this news. Could it be true? Could this whole nightmare be over? He rereads the first few sentences again, rechecking to be sure his mind isn't playing a trick on him.

Eugene Lopez, 58, owner of Lopez Enterprises, was found hanging in his cell Thursday morning, said County Coroner Smith. When guards found Lopez, they cut him down and began CRP and immediately notified medical staff. The inmate was pronounced dead at 7:23 a.m. Lopez was being held on charges related to the sale of drugs and operation of a human trafficking ring. His trial was set for late June. A formal investigation is underway.

"Wow." He agrees with Gabby. "This seems too good to be true."

"Who would have thought?" She leans down to pet Ryder. The dog had been sleeping in his plaid bed in the corner of the room but awakened with all the excitement.

"I know, it's crazy, right? Apparently, Lopez had some other enemies or perhaps other men that he had dealings with thought he would squeal, bringing them down as well."

"This calls for a celebration." Gabby leaves his office but returns with a bottle of tequila in one hand and two shot glasses in the other. The Clase Azul bottle she holds is a classic, ceramic white with hand-painted blue leaves.

Before removing the bell-shaped silver metal cap, she reaches for a pen and gives it a healthy tap. "I love that sound. It brings good luck." Then she pours the clear liquid into the glasses. Handing one to Stan, she makes a toast. "I would never toast to someone's misfortune, even though well deserving; instead, I wish to celebrate a positive so... here's to you."

She lifts her glass. "Stan Adams, rescues woman and is responsible for breaking up a human trafficking operation."

His face turns red as he clicks her glass. He empties the glass. Much to his surprise the tequila burns in his throat but in his stomach, it's warm silk.

"Gabby, there were a lot of people who helped. Your dad for starters. You should have seen him out there in a face-off with Lopez and his men. I was scared shitless but he stood his ground. It was like a modern-day Wild West movie."

"You're right. Daddy was brave." She pours another shot of tequila in both glasses.

"Along with Wayne King, we need to toast to you as well, Gabriella. Yes, Pablo looking down the barrel of Ms. King's gun, sings a confession." He laughs. "Wish I could have seen that one. You and Jamie out there with guns pointed at Pablo and our dear Detective Harrison."

"I refuse to drink to the fine detective. However, I will drink to Daddy, me, and of course, Jamie."

She holds up her glass. "Yes, that was a moment. Got myself landed in jail, a first, and an event I do not wish to repeat. Brett was a bit upset about that one or should I say, really, really, upset but it all worked out. And I got my honeymoon after all."

They click, then drain their glasses a second time. She swallows the tequila, then immediately shakes her hand back and forth.

"Forgot someone." She fills the shot glasses a third time.

He thinks that this celebration is getting out of hand for the middle of a workday, but he'll humor her as it's truly a memorable occasion. He leans back in his chair thinking that she hides this fun side of her personality. Rightfully, she's been through difficult times of her own, long before the Lopez situation, especially with the recent death of her child. He enjoys seeing her vibrant and sparkling.

"We definitely need to toast to Marie, and to Alexa, and to all of the other victims." The song heard on the overhead speakers makes her perk up. "I love this song. Quick, drink up."

They drain the glasses for a third time.

"Dance with me." She walks around the desk and pulls on his arm. "Dance with me, I love this song."

Stan knows from previous events that Gabby is a lightweight when it comes to alcohol. After two glasses of wine at dinner, she'll slur her words a bit. Now after three hits of tequila, she wants to dance. Should he do this? *Careful there, Stan,* an angelic voice in his head warns.

He rises to his feet, allowing her to drag him from the chair. She wraps his arms around her waist, puts hers around his neck, starts to sway in rhythm to the music, and sings along.

Into the second verse, she leans her head into his chest and his heart beats a little bit faster. It feels good to hold her and of course, he'll always love her. It's just the way it is and it will always be. Her head fits beneath his chin and the smell of her Chanel familiar. He's glad that she's a part of his life. It's moments like these: sharing good news, toasting to a success, and caring about each other. He would take this, over having nothing at all in a heartbeat. They're family and this is what family is about.

She stumbles over his shoe and he catches her. "Guess I shouldn't have had that third shot of tequila."

"It's okay, I got you."

She looks up at him, smiling. "I'm glad we're family."

"Me too."

"You're a great guy, Stan. I love you."

"I love you too, sis."

In his thoughts over the past year, he prayed for her to say those words and now that she's said them, it doesn't have the effect that he visualized in those thousand times in his dreams. It was sweet but it wasn't romantic. She loves Brett and maybe he's finally okay with that. He's glad that she thinks him a good person and he prays that she's being honest and it wasn't just the tequila talking. She's family and he's glad he's a part. This impromptu celebration has given him great perspective and for that he is grateful.

CHAPTER 56

San Diego

Marie timidly walks through the automatic sliding glass doors of the hospital. She follows the signs that point to the rehab unit. Her knees are weak and her stomach churns, as she's not certain what she'll find. And will she be brave enough to face her best friend, the girl who was like a sister and whom she hasn't seen in nearly three months? The same person she feels that she's failed. She has a bunch of white daisies in her hand, Alexa's favorite flower.

Their plan for a fun vacation in Cancun turned into a nightmare. She closes her eyes and reminds herself that they're both alive. They survived and even though she wasn't able to help her friend when she was taken from the marijuana farm, they survived because she was brave enough to run—and that escape brought the authorities and saved Alexa.

From what Detective Harrison shared, Alexa suffered greatly both physically and emotionally. This information was confirmed after a call to Alexa's parents. On the phone, the fiftyish woman broke into tears and the father completed the call. Her parents spoke words of gratitude but Marie noted a tone of hardness in their voices as if she is to blame for their daughter's sufferings. Her education as a psychologist gives her an inside view to all of the emotions they must be working through, and she cannot take it personally. As with most things, though, that is easier said than done. It gnaws at her insides, stealing joy that Alexa is alive and in recovery.

Yes, it was her idea to celebrate their graduation with a girls' trip, but how was she to know that it would end this way? It seems from Detective Harrison's description that the woman found in the cathouse was emaciated with needle track marks on both arms. Marie finds it difficult to imagine that her friend with the perfect figure, eyes that shine, and a lively wit, would be reduced to a drug addict with the only thing required for survival being the next fix.

She knows that the use of the drugs is a control factor for the captives but it also is an emotional escape for the victim. It is easier to live with the pleasurable high and hallucinations, instead of facing the painful reality. And the addiction is a chemical dependency that alters the mind. Combining that with the health issues of hepatitis and malnutrition and the emotional trauma with the decline in self-esteem and body image, Alexa has a long road to well-being.

Taking a deep breath to still her apprehensions, Marie approaches the desk outside the double doors blocking passage to the ward.

"Maria Gomez to see Alexa Roberts."

"Ms. Roberts is still in a session. Have a seat." The man motions to a few chairs lined up on the wall opposite. The waiting room is cheery, full of sunlight and in natural colors, inviting the gardens outside to take residence.

She follows his suggestion and picks a chair in the corner. There is one other person in the waiting area, an older woman. She forces a smile but is quick to turn away. She doesn't want to chat. Marie picks up a *Sports Illustrated* and flips through the pages. Pretending to read isn't going to fool anyone, least of all herself. She can't concentrate. She throws the magazine back down on the table, stands, and peers through the glass into the well-groomed, grassy courtyard.

She's wrung so tight she'll snap if she has to wait much longer. Her phone vibrates so she glances at the sender. She ignores the call. It's the second time today that Stan has tried to reach her. She can't speak with him, and what is she to say? She needs to confront the issue that is the cause of her uneasiness; she must talk to Alexa. She needs to apologize. She needs to hug her best friend and reinforce that everything will be all right.

Lost in these thoughts, she's startled when hearing her name.

"Ms. Gomez, good afternoon, I'm Doctor Howard. It's good to meet a friend of Alexa. However, Alexa will not be meeting with you today. I encouraged her that speaking with you would help in her recovery but it seems that she isn't ready to take that step."

His stare is so intense that she looks away.

"It's not in her best interest for anyone to force the issue. She needs to have control. In due time, she'll change her mind. I'm sorry that you came all this way."

"If I saw her, she would change her mind."

"Perhaps, but it's Alexa's decision."

"How is she? Is she getting better?"

"Ms. Gomez, as a professional, you are aware that under privacy laws, I'm not allowed to disclose any information."

Her shoulders slump and she bites her bottom lip and wipes a tear before it travels down her cheek.

"I'm sorry. I can see you care. In due time—perhaps next week." He hands her his card. "Call me before you come. There is one thing that I can suggest that may ease the situation."

She looks up with watery eyes in hope, anticipating his next words.

"Alexa was going to the garden. She spends many hours a day out there." He motions toward the glass. "The garden is part of the facility; however, unless invited, a visitor is not allowed but there's no harm in viewing the beautiful flowers. Some patients, like Alexa, find therapy in gardening. Come with me."

She follows Doctor Howard to the far edge of the window.

"There she is now."

Marie strains to see a small figure kneeling under a large palm at a bed of pink and white begonias. Alexa's back is to her. She gasps at the sight of her friend. She can count the protrusions of Alexa's vertebrae visible under her thin shirt. And why would Alexia cut her beautiful, long hair?

"It is shocking to see the effects of drug addiction," the doctor says as if to comfort.

This time the tears flow and the doctor hands her a tissue. The bouquet she holds shakes, revealing her trembles that she so desperately attempts to hide.

"She's making progress; give it time. I'm hopeful that she'll make a full recovery. Her stint with them, though traumatic, was brief. I've had patients make significant recoveries after years in similar situations. I'm glad you got to see her so that you'll be more prepared the next time." He bows to excuse himself. "It was nice to meet you."

She watches as he leaves. During their exchange, Alexa must have moved. Searching through the glass, bending low, and next on tiptoes peering through the trees and bushes, she's unable to find her friend.

With her head hanging to avoid the stares of passersby, she sees the sliding glass doors to the front of the hospital open and she hurries outside to escape the pain, bathing in the sunlight in an attempt to warm her aching heart. This trip has not turned out as she wished. She dumps her bouquet into the trash, and sits on the steps and cries.

After she regains her composure, she dials a florist and orders an arrangement of daisies to be delivered to Alexa. Then she places a call to Stan.

"It was horrible."

"Hey, slow down." Stan is at the horse center, where he has been speaking with Suzanne. With a wave of his hand, he bids her goodbye and exits the building for privacy. "Take a deep breath and then start at the beginning."

Marie gives him the full account of her visit. He listens and is careful not to interrupt. It was tragic; this entire situation has been traumatic. He's comforted believing that after their call she has placed herself on the right track. It takes nearly an hour for her to give an account of her visit to the rehab unit and her voice quivers when describing Alexa's appearance. However, as the call continues, her voice becomes steadier and stronger. He is moved that she felt comfortable confiding in him and that she called him first.

He's certain that she'll get through this but he didn't predict this severe reaction from the visit. He envisioned that the best friends, after seeing each other, would be so overcome with joy that the tears would fall in thankfulness, not in despair.

Poor Marie—he would like to hold her and tell her that it'll be okay. She has suffered so much. What can he do? He rushes back inside the center to speak with Suzanne before the next patient arrives.

CHAPTER 57

San Diego

S tan searches the ground below. There are a few puffs of white in the azure sky. He checks his watch. The flight from Texas to San Diego is about five hours. He usually naps on a flight but not this one. He takes a sip of the champagne and smiles as the effervescent bubbles hit his upper lip. He's taking a bold step and it's exhilarating.

In a spontaneous act, he's taking King's private KingAir plane to spend the weekend with Marie. He's a bit disappointed that he didn't follow through on reinstating his pilot's license as was his plan after finding the map, but the Lopez situation put his goals on the back burner. King's plane is a beauty and he's anxious to get in the cockpit. The last time he boarded this plane, he was a passenger as well. His mother flew to Washington to bring him to Texas after his motorcycle accident.

He appreciates that Suzanne was able to fill in for him at the horse center so that he could depart early, arriving in time to take

Marie to dinner. It's Friday evening and Old Town will be hopping. He envisions taking her in his arms, laughing, eating, drinking, and dancing. He yearns to know more about this woman who occupies his thoughts dozens of times each day and night.

Yesterday, after their phone call, he sadly became aware that he knows almost nothing about Marie. His knowledge of her is only simple facts. He doesn't know her favorite things: favorite colors, hobbies, flowers. He doesn't know if she prefers horror movies or adventure films. Does she read romance novels or biographies? Does she prefer tequila shots or vodka? There are so many things to learn.

Fondly, he recalls his recent afternoon celebrating with Gabby. He knows so much about Gabby. He's aware of her little quirks and her love for horses, pink roses, and, yes, her love for Brett, but he's now in a place where he can deal with that. He craves to discover similar stuff about Marie and for them to start creating memories together. With Lopez out of the picture, Marie is out of the protective witness program, and he's taking this opportunity to move in. After their evening, he's confident that all of his pressing questions will be answered.

Arriving on a private plane has its advantages, and within minutes he's in a rental car. He crosses the bridge to Coronado Island. He booked a suite at the famous Hotel Del and made reservations at their best restaurant for tomorrow evening. Tonight, he and Marie agreed on a casual Mexican dinner in Old Town. He initially planned to pick her up since he wanted to meet her parents, but she derailed that suggestion and they're meeting at the restaurant. Maybe she thinks meeting her parents premature.

He paces outside the main door of the Mexican Café and rubs his arms in the cool evening breeze. He forgot that the temps here would be cooler than Texas.

Minutes later, he returns from the adjacent shop and resumes pacing in front of the restaurant in a zippered sweatshirt. It's not to his taste but it is practical and comfortable.

"Hey, Stan," she calls as she rounds the building at a fast pace.

She's wearing a long skirt and in the breeze her hair covers her face. He holds open his arms but she stands away as if shy before taking his hand and pecking him on the cheek.

"You look nice."

"So do you. I see you are helping our economy." She points to the logo. "It's common for people to believe it to be warmer. San Diego is south, but the breeze off the ocean keeps it cool. Burgundy suits you."

The restaurant is dark and the candle on the table throws shadows on her face making her expressions harder to read. After ordering and small talk over margaritas, he retrieves a small box from his pocket.

"I bought you a gift." He pushes a brown box tied with a blue ribbon across the table.

"Why?"

"Because a man wishes a woman to have in her possession an item that reminds her of him."

She nods and removes the lid and holds up the single gold chain with a lone dangling star charm. "That's beautiful. Thank you." She holds the bracelet to her arm.

"Allow me the pleasure." He takes the bracelet and secures the clasp, during which his fingers brush the tender skin of her wrist. He makes it a point to rest them there a few seconds before positioning the star on the top. The diamond sparkles in the candlelight.

"It looks expensive. You shouldn't have."

He smiles and takes her hand. "It's a star to remind you of our night. Did you know that when the universe began, when the stars collided millions of years ago, the dust had gold in it? It's amazing to think that something that formed the universe in the very beginning is a part of you and me. Each one of us has a tiny bit of gold inside; truly fascinating."

"That is so beautiful. I never knew."

He gazes into her eyes and sees that she's attentive. He rolls the star, stopping at intervals at the links on the bracelet. "This is a charm bracelet with space for many more charms." He looks down as if paying special attention to the links. "There are hundreds of charms that represent all sorts of things: flowers, hobbies, wishes and dreams." He studies her face.

"After you left, it became clear that I know so little about you. It's sad. I stood at the counter with the saleswoman. She was very enthusiastic, showing me tray after tray holding all sorts of charms, and I went numb. I could not decide. That's when I realized why I couldn't decide. It was because I didn't know much about you." Still holding her hand, he leans across the table.

"I want to know you, Marie. I want to know your favorite color and flower. I want to watch your favorite movie. I want to know what music you play when you jog—or if you jog? I want to stand at that counter, confident and able to buy more charms then the bracelet will hold."

He sits straight but hasn't the nerve to look in her eyes. If he had, he might have seen that she did care and that his gesture and speech touched her deeply.

She squeezes his hand. "Purple... and lilacs. However, they come in to a close second with lily of the valley." She smiles at his thoughtfulness.

"That's a great start. Thank you." He takes a sip of his drink. "Let's enjoy ourselves this weekend. First, tell me about your job search."

The previous tension gone, the two are now chatting away as if they're old friends. When the waitress brings their food, they are in a heavy discussion about which television show or series should win the Emmy Awards next month. Time goes by and after dinner, they walk to a nightclub. They dance and he tries to sing and she laughs. As the clock strikes midnight, he hails a cab and sends her on her way. He doesn't hold a glass slipper but he's certain that his Cinderella will see him again tomorrow.

The following day Marie calls his hotel room before the sun breaks the horizon.

"You up?"

"I am now. What time is it?" He says squinting, searching the numbers on the bedside clock.

"It's morning, silly. I thought we should get an early start."

"Okay, what do you have in mind?" He sits up in the bed.

"You said that you have a motorcycle license. There is a rental place here in town and we can rent bikes and drive north to Julian. Have you ever been there?"

"No."

"Then it's perfect. I'll pick you up in an hour." Before he has time to protest, the receiver blasts a dial tone. He had forgotten that she could ride.

A little over an hour later, Marie and Stan stand inside the rental store. The store has jackets for rent as well as bikes and they are donning leathers for their ride.

"This will be the first time I've ridden since my accident last summer," he says, slipping his arms into the jacket.

She smiles as she loops the strap through the rings on her helmet. "It's about time, then, right?"

"Looking forward to it." He lies as he fakes a smiles and nods. His heart races and the sweat pours down his back.

He wills himself to slow his rapid breathing for fear he will hyperventilate. He wants to ride again but what if he isn't ready? What if his leg hurts and he can't push the clutch and he fails to change gears and...? He has so many fears. He tells himself to ignore these terrifying thoughts and to focus on the positive. He tells himself that getting on a bike is small in comparison to what Marie went through. If she escaped, he can ride a motorcycle, right?

Talking through this strategy works as he bites down hard on his inner cheek and grips the throttle. When she pulls away, he feels he has no choice but to follow. His ego's at stake and he wants to prove he's a survivor.

They spend a delightful day in Julian, a town that was bubbling in the 1870s during the gold rush. They cave in to temptation and participate in several of the tourist attractions. In addition to panning for gold, they take the popular carriage ride.

Afterward on their ride back to the city, they stop at La Jolla and walk the beach. Holding their shoes, so they can feel the sand between their toes, they breathe in the salt air and watch the surfers catching waves.

"Have you ever done that?" She points to one the figures on boards perched momentarily on top of the giant blue crests.

"No," he says.

She pulls his arm so that he faces her. "Not yet, is the better answer. We'll try that the next time you visit." She looks away before he can respond.

He's happy that there will be a next time, but not so much about the idea of surfing. This girl is different than any other that he has dated. Moreover, he likes the way her small frame allows her body to mold into his side when his arm wraps around her. And he likes imagining what she's thinking when she smiles up at him. Once today, after returning the motorcycles, she had that look and said, "I'm proud of you, Stan."

Later that evening, dinner at the Del is everything the critics had reported—gourmet food, exceptional wines, complete with a grand ambiance to help him pop the question.

He clears his throat. "Would you like to spend the night?" His eyes lower in an effort to hide his disappointment if she declines.

However, without hesitation, she says, "Yes."

Her eyes dance, making him wonder why he spent the past few hours turning the words over and over in his mind. He feels like he needed to use the right words and in the right tone or perhaps she might have refused.

Taking a walk after dinner, they stroll along the waterfront and observe the boats, pretending which one they would like to own. They stop at her car as she retrieves an overnight bag from the trunk and he wonders, if he had waited, how she would have worded the offer for them to spend the night together.

After enjoying drinks on the balcony, it's her idea to join him in the shower where she gets the first glimpse of his tattoo. She traces the outline of the blue inked star with her finger and kisses the center. He turns her around taking control and their lovemaking is as steamy as the shower of water that cascades over their slick bodies. She's bold and assertive, and the more he gets to know this woman, the more he appreciates and understands her strong will. And was it this same resilience that saved her? Did her captors sense her strong personality and feel it best for her to work the farm than have her cause trouble in the prostitution ring with influential clients? He has so many questions that still need answers.

CHAPTER 58

Back to Texas

S tan closes his eyes as the plane speeds and he feels the wheels leave the ground. He's on his way back home. He glances to the open seat and thinks that it would have been wonderful if Marie had taken him up on his offer and flown back with him for a few days. He understands her reasons for passing but it would have been great to spend a few more days together.

He smiles as he recalls their weekend. They learned a lot about each other and there were some surprises. In addition to being thoughtful, Marie knows how to encourage others. He took this trip thinking that he was the one able to help her, but it turned out just the opposite. He'd thought he remembered every word she uttered those first two days they spent together when he rescued her, but under those stressful circumstances he had forgotten that she rode motorcycles. Yesterday, her strong will and actions motivated him to face his own fear. It was her idea to ride to Julian.

Now, sitting here on the plane, he's able to smile and be grateful that not only did he ride that motorcycle but he's filled with pride knowing he conquered his fear and the marvelous sense of freedom that riding gave him in the past returned. It was one more step toward getting his former self back or perhaps this new best version of himself. And he has Marie to thank. Gratefulness #1.

Also, the more knowledge he acquires about Lopez and his operation, the more he comes to appreciate the guts it took for Marie to plan and execute her escape. With each passing day that he spends with her, he understands her statement, "I chose to chance dying rather than be a pawn in their evil schemes." When he calculates the odds, it's a miracle that she escaped and that he found her.

Only briefly in their conversations, over the course of the weekend, did Alexa's name come up, and it seems that after getting a glimpse of her in the garden, Marie's handling the situation and understands the importance of giving Alexa the time she needs. Marie shows her support by frequently writing Alexa notes expressing her care and love. It will take time and Marie has patience. The authorities are getting close. Gratefulness#2.

Lastly, he has King to thank as well for helping him regain confidence. King thought him strong enough to face off against Lopez. King risked his life on Stan's ability to hit the targets and explode the Tannerite. King took a huge chance on him and Stan came though. Gratefulness # 3.

As Stan contemplates his life and tallies the three things for which he is grateful, he remembers one more thing that he forgot on this trip—his cane, and he didn't even miss it.

CHAPTER 59

"Hello," Stan yells as he opens the front door carrying his duffel bag. Ryder is the first to greet him.

"Hey, Boss, missed you." He leans down to pet him and allows him to lick his hand.

Rita exits the kitchen, wiping her hands on an apron. "Hi, honey." She gives her older son a hug. "How'd it go? You had a good time?" She stands at arm's length. "I can tell it went well. When you were a little boy, walking home from the bus stop, I could always tell how your day went from the way you walked. Things aren't much different now. You're bigger but it's the same—head held high, smile. Follow me into the kitchen, tell me all about it."

Stan walks to the bar and grabs a longneck from the mini-fridge before following in her footsteps. Ryder's close behind.

"Smells good in here," he says, taking a seat on a counter stool. "Marie was great. We got along great. She loved the bracelet."

"Of course she did, it was beautiful. Did you sleep together?"

"Mother, really? First thing you ask?"

"You can tell me." She stares, waiting for his answer. "I already know, your face is scarlet red."

"Sunburn."

"Sunburn, you say. Can't fool a mother. So how were her parents?"

"Actually, I met them yesterday and they were great. Modest house in an older subdivision. They seemed like really nice people. Her mom's a nurse and her dad is a schoolteacher, teaches high school history. Really down-to-earth people. Marie comes from a good family." He takes a swig of the beer.

"When are you seeing her again?" Rita is making meatballs, rolling them in her hands.

"Not sure. I wanted her to come here for a few days but she says she has a job interview and didn't want to cancel."

"Sounds like she has a good work ethic. That's a good thing. Long-distance relationships are tough."

"We talked about that. She could look for a job here or I could move out there."

Rita stops rolling her meatball and raises her eyebrows.

"It's too early to make any long-term plans. We're taking it slow."

"Um-hum, so you say."

He throws a dish towel at her. "Hey, why are you cooking?"

"With you gone, and Brett and Gabby staying in town for the weekend, Jamie and Rusty took a little vacation—a well-deserved vacation. They went to Galveston to enjoy the beach...before it gets busy around here again."

"Oh, busy how?"

"Your brother and Ella are coming on Friday. What's that thing you young people do these days? You know, where you take that last vacation before the baby arrives."

He walks over to the stove and stirs the spaghetti sauce. "A baby-moon."

"Yes, that's it, a babymoon. Ella wants to see her mom and dad, and we haven't seen them either since the holidays. They're going to stay with Gabby and Brett since they have a spare room. I thought we'd throw them a baby shower." She places the tray of meatballs into the oven. "There that's done."

"Where's King?"

"Down at the barn. Seems he likes that little office he set up down there for himself when you were in his study. You want to tell him to get washed up for dinner?"

"Sure. I need to tell him thanks for the plane. It was pretty awesome. Flying around like I'm somebody."

"Of course you're somebody. Don't you forget that." She hugs him and kisses him on the cheek. "I'm happy your weekend went well."

"Me too, Mother." He turns to go out the kitchen door on his way to the barn.

CHAPTER 60

Equine Center

The next day Stan is at the Equine Center, opening the office for the day. Gabby stands in his doorway. "Damn, did you know this?"

"I just got here, same as you, so that would be an honest no." He can't imagine what could have happened since he was gone only for a three-day weekend. Everything was in order when he left the center on Thursday afternoon.

She throws a letter down on his desk. "Suzanne's leaving the agency and taking a full-time position, some new place opening up south of the city." She puts her left hand on her hip. "We should have offered her a job. She was the best therapist. She was getting to know the horses and she's so good with the patients. In a month, she starts her new job. We'll have to train someone else. Start all over. Who will we find that has such a sweet voice and sings in French? I love listening to her."

"I see." He rubs his chin as he scans the letter. "Suzanne is good.

We could make her a better offer. Let me check the numbers and I'll see what's the best we can come up with and still stay in the black. Right now we go through an agency, but if we hire Suzanne outright, we'll need to consider benefits such as holidays and health care, and weigh that against the fee we pay the agency. It could be close to the same. I'll get on it right away."

"You know, you're to blame." She points a finger at him. "Yep, I can't be certain but I do have a theory."

"What? You have a theory as to why Suzanne is leaving?"

"She's leaving because of you."

He rolls his eyes. "You can't be serious. I didn't do anything."

"My point—you didn't do anything. Men are so clueless." She throws her hands up in the air. "She likes you. She's liked you for a while now and you barely gave her the time of day. Then you go off to California to visit your Marie, and you ask Suzanne to cover for you. She got pissed and typed this letter."

"You're delusional."

"Think about it, Stan. How many times did Suzanne come into your office to ask you questions? How often did she invite you for a drink after work?"

"Her questions were about work. It had nothing to do with me." He leans back in his chair.

"Like I said, men are clueless. She would come into your office to spend time with you, silly. But ever since you found Marie, she's all you talk about, Marie this and Marie that. The poor girl couldn't take it anymore."

"Like I said, you can't be serious."

"Poor Stan, women falling all over you...Suzanne... Marie. You really don't know how to play the field, do you?"

"Guess I'm just an old-fashioned boy." He sits up straight in his chair and smiles. Watching Gabby compares to watching a performance on stage. Entertainment at its best.

"Guess you are...one of the few good ones left." She walks behind him and pats him on the back. "Glad you had a good weekend." She winks. "When you have those numbers, let me know, but if you'd be uncomfortable with Suzanne working here, we need to figure something else out. Okay, Casanova." She clicks her tongue, turns and leaves.

CHAPTER 61

King Ranch

It's Sunday morning and the King men are out on an early ride through the pastures and trails of the ranch. Today is Will's second time riding horseback. The first time he was on a horse was last spring when he visited the ranch for his mother's wedding.

"I forgot how beautiful it is here," Will says, his lean frame sitting tall in the saddle. "The sky is bigger and much bluer than in Washington."

"No smog out here and of course it's bigger since everything's bigger in Texas," Stan is eager to reply.

"You're riding like you know what you're doing there, big brother. I'll never forget the day last year when you walked in the door after you had fallen. I'm just sorry Gabby didn't snap a photo." Will laughs.

Overhearing the conversation, King rides up between the brothers. "Stan's worked really hard these past few months. We're very proud of him. He's almost a real cowboy."

"Hey, what do you mean almost? I got my boots, my Stetson, and these gloves show wear after helping with the cattle drive."

This time it's Brett who answers, "You look the part, but for real cowboy status, you need to rope a cow."

"I can do that." Stan smiles at Rusty and he winks. "I've watched you, Mr. Rodeo, many a time so I've been learning from the best."

"Damn straight. Thanks, Stan. Maybe when we get back, we can give you a chance." He tips his hat.

"You're on." Stan looks to Rusty and Rusty gives a nod.

While the men are riding, the King women are having coffee on the porch, during which Ella finishes opening her gifts from yesterday's baby shower.

Since Ella and Will arrived via the airport on Saturday, the baby shower at a downtown restaurant was the perfect plan. However, with so much conversation between all the guests, Ella abandoned opening her gifts in favor of catching up on the latest news.

Now on the porch, her feet surrounded by wrapping paper and ribbons, Ella holds up a little lavender dress for the rest to see.

"Thank you, Rita, for arranging the shower. It was very sweet and totally unexpected. I loved seeing all of my sorority sisters again. So much has happened in these past ten years since graduation. Go, Horns." Ella makes the hand sign of the university with her forefinger and little finger sticking up in the air. "Those were some great times." She shakes her short dark hair.

"They sure were. Best memories ever," Gabby says as she gathers the discarded paper, placing it into a garbage bag. "I think that was the last of them—presents, not the memories. Girlfriend, you and I are going to continue making great memories." Then they do their secret sorority handshake, followed by giggles. "Strange how things have a way of working out. My best friend is married to my stepbrother. It's perfect." Gabby leans down and gives Ella a hug. "It won't be long until we have a little sister in our circle."

"Laura," Ella says. "Her name will be Laura, after Will's grand-mother."

With this bit of news, Rita jumps out of her chair and clasps her hands together. "Awesome, you made this grandmother-to-be very happy."

Ella holds on to her baby bump. "As soon as I mentioned the name to Will, he loved it and refused to discuss any other, so Laura it is."

"I hear the horses. I'll go and help them so we can get brunch started. I'm starved so I'm sure they are as well." Gabby hops off the porch and heads to the barn as Rita and Jamie help Ella pack up the baby gifts.

"What's going on?" Gabby asks, rounding the corner. The men have brought some calves back with them.

"Stan's going to become a real cowboy today." King says, dis-mounting Diesel.

She furls her brow.

Brett leads Frog over to the trough before embracing Gabby. "Stan is going to rope a calf—an act to obtain official qualifying rights to cowboy status. "

"Now? On a Sunday?"

King leads the calves into the corral. "No time like the present. Stan here wants to show off for his little brother. Ain't that right?"

"Sunday, fun day," Brett sings. Will laughs.

Gabby puts her hands on her hips. "Stan, you don't have to do this. They're teasing you."

"I want to do this."

"This is ridiculous. Who made up such a thing?" She surveys the four men.

King laughs. "That would be your husband. We're just having some fun."

"You shouldn't have fun at the expense of another...that's bullying. Stan..." She turns to him expecting him to call it off.

"I got this. Relax, little sis." Stan smiles and shakes his head, amused at her attempts to defend his honor.

"What about brunch?'

"It will still be there. Tell Jamie to hold off making those hotcakes." King removes the saddle from Diesel.

"Men sure have weird ideas." She dials Rita informing her of the delay.

Rusty has the calves in the corral and Stan practices his cutting technique. Brett gives some helpful hints as he leans on the fence with Gabby by his side.

"This is insane." She bites her fingernails.

"He'll be fine." Brett puts his arm around her. "Hey, Stan, get that calf in a bit closer to the fence," he yells as he squeezes her shoulder.

Stan looks around the outer fence of the corral where his mother has joined the rest of the family. The gloves hide his sweaty hands and he looks up to the promising blue skies in an act of gratefulness, filling his lungs with the fresh air. He has done this successfully a dozen times but he has also missed. With a less than fifty percent success rate, the odds are not in his favor. However, if he misses the first try, no big deal; he'll try again. And if he misses that time, he'll remain calm and try again. He has a plan, but the likelihood that he never ropes a calf is small.

Rusty pats him on the thigh. "Son, just like we practiced. Got it?"

Stan nods and makes certain the head rope is free of kinks. Then he lowers it, ensuring the noose has the proper kick and the honda knot slides with ease. Confident the equipment is unflawed, he gives Rusty the ready sign to run the calf.

Stan kicks his horse in the chase. Swinging the lasso with a helicopter motion when it gains a forward momentum, he releases, then moves his hand around to grab the slack. As the calf is roped, around the corral a cheer erupts.

The initial challenge complete but with adrenalin peaking, Stan has more to prove. He dismounts, grabs the calf's flank and flips him over. Even Stan is surprised at the ease with which the calf turns. Quickly he grabs his tie-down rope from his belt, and with a wrap and a slap, the calf's three legs are secured. Stan throws his arms up in the victory sign, his face beaming.

Straightaway, Brett crawls into the corral and attempts to pick him up. Watching, Will, and King join in and together they lift Stan up and twirl him around.

"That performance won't win you a buckle at the rodeo but you did all right, man. Impressive," Brett says.

Will says, "Guess you are a real cowboy. Who would have thought?"

Gabby and Rita join the celebration and after Rita finished congratulating Stan, Gabby hugs him close and whispers in his ear, "Way to show them, champ." Then smacks a kiss on his cheek.

Jamie emerges from around the corner. "Isn't anyone hungry?"

"Guess we'd better get a move on. Don't want to upset the cook," King says, waving to Jamie. "We'll be right there."

CHAPTER 62

King Ranch

With the morning activities, Sunday brunch at the King ranch house is finally underway. After King's tradition of saying grace, he raises his glass. "A toast to having our family together." He pauses and gestures toward the young couple, Ella and Will. "And to the arrival of the little one who will be joining us in a few months."

"Here, here," Rita chimes in. "To Laura."

The glasses click all around. Then King adds more. "To Stan for his heroic efforts—saving women in distress, capturing evil men, reaching real cowboy status, and I hear from the womenfolk, a sort of Casanova." King bows in respect to Stan. "Oh to be young."

Stan feels the heat rising above his collar as the others turn to him.

King pauses a few seconds enjoying Stan's reaction. "After dinner, we men will be retreating to the study for an official celebration."

Rita looks to King as if she doesn't understand.

"An official celebration with The Cowboy."

"Wayne, what does that mean? That's not some other silly initiation."

"No, my love, not to worry." He squeezes her hand. "The Cowboy—it's a bourbon distilled just west of here and its promoted to be…strong enough to run a car with an incredibly smooth finish. I save it for special occasions. Brett and I opened the bottle last December after he placed in the National Rodeo and today, we are going to finish that bottle celebrating Stan's status to real cowboy—with no other than The Cowboy." He pats his wife's hand again. "Makes perfect sense to me." He chuckles. "I love my family. Thank you, all of you, thank you."

Gabby isn't certain but she thinks she caught a glimmer of a tear resting in the corner of her father's eye and Stan's face seems to beam like the morning sun.

CHAPTER 63

Equine Center

Stan throws the newspaper down on his desk before turning to speak to Ryder. "It's good to be back at work, right, Boss?"

Ryder sniffs around the office until he finds his pull toy behind the door and lays it at Stan's feet.

"Sorry, pal. I got work to do."

Ryder lays back his ears, sits, and chews on the toy. The center has a full schedule. Even with an improved contract, Suzanne didn't accept their offer, leaving them in search of a new psychologist. In the following weeks the agency sent several therapists, but both Stan and Gabby agree that none felt like the perfect fit and they should continue the search.

Gabby left him a message early this morning texting that another therapist is starting today for a two-week probationary period. A new therapist always means more work for both of them as there's an orientation process, and many questions to answer. Stan shakes his head, realizing that he'll need some additional coffee.

Exiting his office for the kitchenette down the hallway, he grinds his coffee beans, scooping them into the pod for the Keurig. Waiting for the coffee to brew, a loud bang that seems to have come from the psychologist's office is bothersome. He thought he was the first to arrive at the center. Curious, he leaves his brewing coffee and goes to investigate. Opening the door, there are books sprawled over the floor and a woman crouches over a box picking them up.

"Here, let me help you with that." Stan rushes forward and as she turns to face him, he stops in his tracks.

"I'm sorry...oh, Stan, good morning." She smiles.

"Marie?" He rocks back on his heels.

"Gabby didn't tell you. She wasn't sure that she should, and from your expression she didn't. I applied for the position. I'm the new therapist." She stands and brushes her pants. "There's a probationary period so if it doesn't work out, there'll be no hard feelings. Okay?" She pushes her hair behind her ear.

"I'm getting really nervous here. Stan...please say something, anything." She wrings her hands.

Stan takes her in his arms, lifting her feet off the floor, and twirls her around. "I can't believe you're here." Then he steps back. "But you don't know anything about horse therapy."

"I didn't. When I was put into protective custody, I asked to be placed as an intern at a center in southern California. The feds rejected that idea, not because of the therapy but because of the location, thinking it too close to home. However, they found me a school in Wyoming. I completed a six-week course and I loved it. I was hurting so much inside that by learning about the horse therapy, I was healing as well. I confided in one of the instructors, and he used the techniques on me.

"Nothing compares to understanding, then going through a situation yourself. That horse saved me. In those short weeks, I was on both the receiving end and then the teaching end. So here I am. I got my certificate, framed and ready to be nailed on the wall behind this desk. And these books," she points to the scattered piles on the floor, "I brought them all, including my stargazers guide, so I'm going to try really hard to make this work. It was your suggestion that I look for work in Texas. So, here I am. Tell me what you think." Her hands are on her hips.

"I'm in shock and I don't know what to say. Wow...why didn't you tell me when I came to San Diego?"

"I still had to take my exams. I wanted it to be a sure thing before mentioning it. Say it's a great idea. Say congratulations. Say that you missed me." She reaches for his hands. "After you left, I realized I know so little about you. I want to know your favorite color, your favorite season of the year, and your favorite food."

He fingers the bracelet on her wrist and faces the star upward. "Blue, spring, and pot roast...and I missed you. I really missed you." He buries his nose in her hair that smells of coconut and pulls her in tight. "Best day at the office ever."

Acknowledgements

It is a pleasure to write the acknowledgements for the first book in The KNOT Series II. If you remember, I had mixed feelings with the ending of the first series. I was happy to complete the third book but at the same time I was sad because the characters had more growing to do and more life's lessons to learn. Stan was one of these characters. I hope that his story proved inspiring. As we all should live our true selves, Stan learned to find his unique gifts and this is what made him shine. Can you reflect on your life and think of the gifts that have caused you to shine?

I also wrote this story to bring an awareness to the horrific crime of human trafficking.

I can be contacted at www.donnaleeoverly.com and as always your review on Amazon and GoodReads is always a blessing.

This book would not have been possible without the help of many others and I am extremely grateful. Thank you to girlfriends who listened and provided insight, the experts who shared their precious knowledge, my beta readers and my understanding editor and friend, Emily Carmain, and Roseanna White for cover design.

A special note of thanks to my family for putting up with me: my husband for his continuous love and support of my hobby, and to my son, Dan, for saving my manuscripts
(just in case I crash my computer) and advice.
Love you!
DonnaLee

Don't miss DonnaLee Overly's next book,

The second book in

The Knot Series II

Coming Fall 2021

True Love Knot

CPSIA information can be obtained
at www.ICGtesting.com
Printed in the USA
LVHW041357141120
671373LV00003B/147